CW01500635

ALL CREATURES
LIVING BENEATH
THE SUN

Enjoy this author-curated playlist as you read.

ISBN (paperback): 978-1-959153-05-4
ISBN (eBook): 978-1-959153-06-1

This is a work of fiction. Names, places, characters and incidents
are either the product of the author's imagination or are used
fictitiously, and any resemblance to any actual persons, living or
dead, organizations, events or locales is entirely coincidental.

Printed in the United States of America.

Published by

www.albatrossbookco.com

C.S. FRITZ PRESENTS

ALL CREATURES LIVING BENEATH THE SUN

For my mother,
who never discouraged my macabre sensibilities.

AUTHOR NOTE

*The unrealistic nature of these tales
is an important device, because it makes
obvious that the fairy tales' concern is not useful
information about the external world, but the
inner process taking place in an individual.*

—Bruno Bettelheim,
*The Uses of Enchantment: The Meaning
and Importance of Fairy Tales*

MY HEART HAS ALWAYS BENT TOWARD the collision of the innocent and grim. The majority of my storytelling career has been in the genre of children's storybooks, mostly concentrated on fairy tales. These kinds of stories are like hard candy being plucked from a witch's house. They must be savored. The consumer must slow themselves while digesting all that comes from them because there are lessons to be gleaned from children climbing beanstalks to giant lairs or the occasional puppet transforming into a boy. Viewing the world through the eyes of innocence allows the vehicle of macabre or fanciful storytelling to enrich the reading experience. It enables a pure reading of the tale and elevates the stakes of the story arcs. This is why I continually write from the vantage of a candle in the dark, a child in the woods, or a wish in a well.

One story in particular has always blurred the trinitarian lines between evil, truth, and myth: The Pied Piper of Hamelin. A *true* horror story. If you haven't read it yet, you can find the poem at the end of the book. A small town with a large rat infestation promises to pay a certain piper to remove the rats. The piper does this with a musical charm, calling the rats to follow his song. The townspeople decide to not pay, and the piper then plays his song one last time, calling this time all the town's children to himself. The children are never to be seen again. Now, if you study the history of this fairy tale, you will discover a treasure trove of lore and enchantment. For generations, many have said it is based in truth, that the great children's crusade was in fact true. But, I read one ancient account that put hot coal in my chest . . . It said every child was lured by the piper *except three.*

One blind child, one deaf child, and one lame child. Once I discovered this, the story you are about to read came ablaze within me.

Could I write a version of this antiquated tale from their challenged perspective?

Could I write a story that stays true to the tale but increase the experience of reading it by adding darkness to darkness?

Could I write something brutal, original, and viciously disturbing yet still have one foot in the country of a well-known myth?

Well, I guess I'll allow you to judge that. Friends, readers, pilgrims, storytellers . . . I give you *All Creatures Living Beneath the Sun*, a cruel retelling of The Pied Piper myth.

Consider this your trigger warning,
— C.S. FRITZ

I'm able,

By means of a secret charm, to draw

All creatures living beneath the sun,

That creep or swim or fly or run,

After me so as you never saw!

—The Pied Piper of Hamelin

PROLOGUE

THE HOUSE SAT ON MORE ACREAGE than one could fathom. Wild horses on the back end, rivers to the east. It was all theirs. A spot of land no one could take. A bosom of perceived happiness and warm meals, a place where angels have no reason to visit. Their home was erected in the center of pastureland, fixed with black shutters, high windows, and a large, wooden porch where the family often congregated in the summer months. But like an urn on the mantle, these rooms held their secrets, and their closets harbored their trespasses.

This is why.

This is why the home in the center of the pastureland was now consumed in by fire. A purification.

Windows popped open like embers, doors fell from searing hinges, porch stairs curled heavenward. Though the family possessed everything, in death it was placed upon the altar, skinned from them as they unwillingly entered the narrow door of eternity.

Naked we come, and naked we are sent.

Spurts and crackles continued to collapse the family home, wormholes where shingles used to lay, dismemberment where beating hearts once drummed, tears where laughter once came. From the front door, life emerged from the flames like a phoenix from hell. Blasted, kicked from its innards, birthing a flame child of its own, a young boy burst from the gut of the fiery home, fully engulfed. Beneath the tangerine sky now billowing with acrid smoke was a marmalade inferno incarnated in a young boy.

The child was on fire, a crown of flame flowering from his head. His fire looked like angel wings resting upon his shoulders and quickly melting back, flapping in the night sky. His skin slumped to the dirt beneath him, globs of cooked skin plopped and baked to the ground as it dripped from his body. The fire boy ran frantically, holding something precious to his chest. Rather than extinguishing the fire or rolling in the cool mud, the child, ablaze, fell to his knees and hacked at the earth with a bloodied kitchen cleaver, as if cursing the dust from which he came. His mission, greater than his life, seized his entire spirit. Not a haunting, not a possession, but a second birth.

"Hurry, star-watcher!" His hand said to him as the autonomous limb watched the digging process. "There isn't much time," it continued. His fingers formed a perfect beak shape, darting between the boy's face and the hole, spewing directions. The fire child's hand had no eyes, but he could feel it watching his every move with increasing intensity. "Don't let her down!" it yelled. With renewed zeal, he dug at the ground frantically over and over with both hands. The dig was so intoxicating, the fire boy didn't notice the blossoming dandelions creeping up around where he knelt. The earth beneath him was lit, and his body performed like a candle to the dark forest surrounding him. Now at full height, the dandelions emitted a fluorescent glow, the colors reminding him of Indian summers. His hands moved with precision. Up down, up down. Faster. Deeper. The invisible dictator shouted words of strained encouragement,

FIRE BOY

despite having no teeth, lips, or tongue to be found. But the boy could feel it. He could hear it. As it tried to swallow and breathe, the wrist expanded and deflated with every breath. "I'm trying!" the child screamed at his hand.

"Faster, faster, faster!" His fleshy, fingered sock puppet barked back.

"I'm dying! Help me," the boy said, feeling his body begin to betray him.

"Pathetic," the hand said, turning up to the boy's face like a disgruntled parent. "Maybe we should have looked for another?"

Those words were too much to bear for the burning child who had sacrificed everything. He raised the discarded cleaver and brought it down upon the wretched talking hand, leaving the fire boy a boned stump. Blood surged, the pain slow to come, as it mixed with the reddish, iron-rich dirt, rendering the ground pliable. The fire child didn't make a peep, as even in his dying he rather enjoyed the silence. Blessed silence. Alone with his thoughts at last.

When the flames thawed the ground enough to carve, he scooped it and pulled it to his knees, cooling his hot, gooey skin. He shooed away the wriggling fingertips of his friend and placed the sacred treasure he'd set nearby in its new residence, laying the old earth back upon it. Tufty white pappi from the dandelions fluttered in the air with the commotion, where they sizzled in the fire that licked his skin. Before his imminent death, the boy prostrated himself once more on the treasure mound and mumbled three times words too faint to hear.

A secret between him and the gods.

Prayers of a hopeful demon.

A wish.

PART one

"IT'S BEEN SAID THAT no matter where you are, you're always near a rat having sex."

"No fucking way, Dot! That can't be true," Wentworth said as he pulled himself from leaning against the school's stone wall. A sign of his full attention. "I'm just telling you what I be reading. And rats are always having sex, and that's why there are so many of them," Dot said more firmly this time, but with a small, smug smile poking through. She never smiled as much as she did when talking about sex, blood, or buttholes.

Archie tugged on Dot's shirt to have her write on his chalkboard whatever she was filling Wentworth's brain with. She shrugged Archie off as she watched Wentworth ready his grist. He adjusted the cloth bandage around his eyes and hammered his walking cane into the ground like a wizard. The snow beneath their feet crunched with the smack of the cane, making a small puff of fresh snow with each step.

"Wait, wait, wait!" he yelled with delighted horror. "Are you telling me babies come from sex? Like I'm here, 'cause some mum and pop humpty-dumptied, and I popped out like a gumball?" He had always imagined humans sprung from large eggs, robin's egg blue for boys and tongue pink for girls. At least, that's what he'd been told. He wasn't entirely sure he knew what blue or pink even was. His imagination was stern enough, though. Mothers would lay their warm bodies on them eggs, waiting for the tapping and cracking. But never sex! Wenty silently cursed his biology and anatomy teachers at Blackburn's for failing him in this most crucial area. Or maybe he just hadn't been listening that day. He did have a habit of letting his thoughts wander. When you're blind, your thoughts are your lifeline.

"Holy fuck, Wenty. Are you telling me you didn't know sex makes rat babies? Yes, your mum and dad fiddled, and you were shit out the second it was done. Whiskers and all. That's the circle of life," Dot exclaimed as she took a wooden pipe from beneath the plaid blanket on her lap, tamping its tobacco and lighting it like a seasoned furloughed sailor. Her fingertips turned purple in the winter air. She hoped the warmth from her bowl would heat them up. Dot knew smoking pipes was silly for a twelve-year-old girl to do, but so was sitting in a wheelchair. Dot's existence was bent on getting the short end of the stick or soup with flies in it. Smoking was one of the few things she could control in her life. The amount of tobacco to pack, the number of puffs to suck, how many matches to strike. These were her choices. "Every woman's butt sneezes out a baby after the man puts a tadpole inside of her. Duh," Dot said, exhaling gray dragon's breath, a mixture of smoke and condensation from the cold.

Archie's eyes were the size of cheese wheels. He could see Dot and Wenty were on to something big. It didn't help that instead of writing it on the chalkboard that dangled from his neck, Dot kept taking her finger and jamming it into the hole her other hand had made. She laughed hysterically, making Wenty squirm and pound his walking stick against her wheelchair. Nonetheless, Archie joined in the laughter, fully unaware of the joke. This is what Archie was best at, going with the tide, never against it. A boy made of sand, washed to and fro. Something he knew himself but was too afraid to allow others to realize. He'd often send out prayers for purpose, although unspoken. He knew no one was listening. To him, the world was just as deaf as his own ears.

Moments of silence filled the air like the falling snow as they watched each other catch snowflakes in their mouths. In these moments, Wenty would often stand there with his pink tongue erect, waiting for an unexpected flake to fall into his gaping hole. Dot would notice and blow some flakes toward him, to no avail. She'd grab Wentworth's hand and place her hot pipe into it, allowing him to take a long drag. This both amused and distracted him, for which he was thankful.

Dot snatched Archie's chalkboard from around his neck and placed it on her paralyzed lap. As she set it down, her fingers grazed her knee, reminding her for a moment of her shrinking bones, her useless limbs. She drew a pair of rats doing each other.

Archie would never tell her, and Wentworth would never see it, but Dot was an amazing artist. Even a couple of rats screwing in scribbles was somehow beautiful to Archie. If he didn't need his chalkboard for communication, he'd have framed it.

"That one kinda looks like Puck, don't you think?" Dot asked Archie.

Archie's deaf ears were confused by Dot's jumbled words as she spoke with the pipe hanging out of her mouth. Dot wrote "P u C K" in large letters on the chalkboard, ruining her art. Wentworth chuckled as he attempted to blow smoke rings into the air, imaging they were Viking horses.

Archie waved his chubby hands as if to swat the thought away and reached into his top jacket pocket, pulling a black rat seemingly from within himself. There Puck sat, nibbling on a piece of twine.

"Keep that thing away from me!" Wentworth yelled, patting the pipe ashes into the schoolyard. Wenty had never actually seen a rat, but his fear of them was palpable. He'd been told of their pricked teeth and hairless pink tails and their ability to chew through baby bones. But there was something deeper to his unease than his own imagination. Dot and Archie just didn't know what. Something about the way they moved. Always in the shadows, lurking, scurrying, and taking whatever they could find. Never giving. Because of Wenty's increased sense of awareness and hearing, he was subject to increased exposure to these creatures' wanderings and shrill squeaks and hisses as they flowed about the old school walls and hallways. The sound would be deafening at times for the blind boy. Thanks to Sister Margaret's deft animal biology lecture, he also knew that these rodents couldn't see very well, only being able to focus about one or two feet in front of them at any given moment. They often relied on shapes and sounds in the distance to detect movement or danger, just like Wenty.

"Relax, bird dick," Dot said, reaching to rub Archie's pet.

"Have you told him yet what we heard Sister Margaret talking about?" Wentworth asked, sucking the lightheartedness out of the air like tobacco.

"Not yet," Dot said, watching Archie with disgust and pity as he pet and kissed Puck with tender affection.

Puck hated the cold and often hid in the boy's jacket when the children were outside. "It'll destroy him, and that'll destroy me."

Wentworth could tell by the maternal tone of her voice that she saw Archie as a child. Her child. He couldn't tell if their relationship made him jealous or angry. Or both. These were the moments he was grateful for his darkened eyes and inability to confirm what he believed to be true. Wentworth tapped his fingers against his cane as if they were snares for a firing squad. He'd tell Archie himself if he had any way to communicate with him. He could never see what he was writing.

"Dot," Wenty said, handing her back her pipe, "don't you think that's a bit—"

"Selfish?" Dot interrupted.

Wenty pinched his lips together. He knew in his gut he didn't have the courage to tell his friend the truth.

"It is selfish. Can't I be selfish about this one thing? Fuck," Dot said painfully, unlocking her wheelchair. "Forget it. I gotta go to the nursery. I'm already late."

"Dot, I didn't mean to upset you, but he'll find out soon enough. Better it comes from us," Wentworth said, reaching for her chair to reposition himself to be sure he was still speaking to her head-on.

"I know, I know. Soon they'll all be killed, and that'll kill him."

"And good riddance, but I don't want Archie to be hurt or act different because of it," Wentworth snarled back. The three left their hiding spot, forging their way back into what others would call home. They thought of it more as a cell. Dot looked up as she glided beneath the school's ancient stone arches. She made her way to the nursery to help the sisters with the orphaned infants. Forgotten saints and crumbling gargoyles looked down upon her from their cold posts. For years, she laughed at the thought that they were guarding her or keeping her prisoner. But she'd abandoned those sorts of thought experiments. It was better for her this way.

Caged.

Clipped wings.

This is what Blackburn's does, she thought. *This is what it is. A crumbling stone nest for broken birds and rats.*

GIRL WHO COULDN'T WALK

BLACKBURN'S WAS LOCATED EXACTLY fifty-three miles outside of Hanover. Originally a thriving parish built long ago, it was complete with towering spires and old cathedral-style ceilings. One could easily see it was once a staple in the community. A towering safe-haven for the people living in its holy shadow. At some point, the town dispersed, be it from famine or sickness, and the church fell to ruins with the souls of the people. The paint was peeling, the stained glass was broken, and all manner of vermin and mildew crept in and took residence.

Decades later, a venal mayor saw it as the perfect fit for the country's growing number of orphans. The hefty appropriation that came along with hosting such a crew was too good to pass up. So a local parish was enlisted to run the Catholic boarding school that was hurriedly retrofitted for the deranged, broken, unwanted children in the country. Nearly every

year, thirty to fifty "trash babies" were dropped—
or thrown—from carriages upon the stone doorstep
of this school. This prison. It's where home, hell,
and refuge intersected. A place where both angels
and demons come to play and fuck. But, besides
the seemingly mutant children who live there and
the hypocritical authority who runs it, the rats now
play god.

"Our rodent problem has gotten worse."

The words lay in the office like dense fog. Hard
to see or know anything else through its gray.

"Not this again. We've gone over this before.
I couldn't afford to do anything years ago, and I
can't now."

"Worthless!" Sister Margaret shouted as she
slammed her fist on the mayor's desk, rattling his
trinkets and frames. Sister Margaret eyed the wooden
frame containing the mayor's perfect family—his
children and their pastel smiles. The nun wasn't used
to seeing children smile.

"Jesus, Margaret, we just don't have the budget
for it. You know this," he said, quieting the desk
ornaments.

The nun came back to the moment. "We don't

ask for help. We don't ask for money or food. The last time we came knocking on your door was over ten years ago, about that poor baby's eyes, which were . . . Well, you know," she said, covering her throat. "So here we are again. Do you know what results from an infestation of rats?" she asked with a high brow.

"Sister—"

"I came all this way, at least do me the decency of answering me. Or pretending to give a shit."

The expletive brought the mayor's eyes to meet the sister's. "I can only imagine," he said, offering the sister a drink of aged whiskey.

"Then you can imagine the severity of the infestation," Sister Margret said, taking the tumbler without hesitation.

The mayor picked at the edge of his glass, avoiding eye contact. "Sister Margaret, the government appreciates your ministry. This isn't about us ignoring you. This is about our budget, which we do not have."

Sister Margaret half-listened as she watched the golden and rubied rings that danced around the mayor's fat, manicured fingers.

"How bad can it be? The school is quite large. Can you move the children to a different wing?" he offered.

The nun lowered her eyes, rubbed her forehead, which sat snug under her pressed coif, and slammed her drink on the desk. "A different wing, you said?" The sister repeated.

The mayor could see the frayed edges at the end of her cincture. What was once a prided sign of distinction had become dirtied, sullen, and worn with daily workload. A real-life metaphor for the school's current state. This was her last hope. She was, literally and figuratively, at the end of her rope. Sister Margaret bent over, swaying her black habit to the side as she rummaged through something out of sight. The mayor leaned over his large oak desk, attempting to see the way a child might peek at a magician's trick.

Thunk! Sister Margaret dropped the burlap bag onto his desk. Its stains and stench puddled the air.

"And what is this?"

The nun gave a smirk, untied the bag, and allowed its contents to land heavily on the mayor's desk. From the bag poured several dead cats.

Each cat was missing its ears, eyes, and nose. The cavities of their bodies had been licked clean, even cleaner than the matted fur that dangled from their bones. The stench wasn't coming from the bodies themselves, but the rat shit that painted them. Droppings in clusters the size of coins stuck to each of them like boils. "Last week, we adopted over thirty mousers, trained barn cats, and hunters. This is them now, mayor. I couldn't grab the rest because they were just blobs of fur and innards. Ghosts of what used to be. But if you'd like, I could go back and retrieve them for your review," the nun added with cutting sarcasm.

"Good god," the mayor said, using his silk tie to cover his mouth and nose.

"Yes, he is, but this has nothing to do with him. This is the work of Satan himself. Devil-rats. I'll be back, mayor," the nun said, wiping her hands off with her habit. "Either you get me the extermination we need, or we will be forced to drop off each and every child at the school on your doorstep. Did I mention we have over one hundred and forty children with us now?"

With that, the door closed, leaving the mayor with a table full of dead cats.

A DISHEVELED CARRIAGE PULLED UP in front of Blackburn's before breakfast. Archie knew this because his entire day orbited three crucial events: breakfast, lunch, and dinner. Dot and Archie stared out the window as Dot described the scene to Wenty in Dickens-like detail. "It's the same carriage as last week, the one with broken windows and the driver whose face looks like pudding."

"And . . . and how many kids do you see?"

"Only one as of now. Another boy. This one with red hair."

"Describe red again," Wenty asked as his heels went up and down.

Dot looked down, allowing her mind to try and find descriptors like a rat searching for cheese. She struggled when he asked her to describe colors. "Ummm, red looks like danger. It feels hot to look at, as if it could warm or hurt you." In her heart, she desperately wanted to share the world she saw with the boy who couldn't see. She seized every chance, no matter how preoccupied she might be, to widen his world of darkness.

Wenty allowed his head to rest upon the damp stone wall behind him as his mind struggled to imagine such a color. He often allowed his mind's eye to enrapture him, consuming the moment for an epiphany of sight. He loved the way Dot described the world to him. Her words were his eyes. When Dot allowed it, Wenty pleaded with her to describe the shape of rain, freckled cheeks, or the hue of skin. But alas, he regained composure, whispering, "Tell me about his face!"

Archie turned around and glanced at the other two, his face sweaty and bright as if holding a secret. Mondays were filled with angst and were easily the group's favorite day of the week. *Ramp Day*, as it was coined by the administration, was the day freshly admitted misfits were brought to their new home. Or rather, their new inferno. But the residents, including Dot, Archie, and Wentworth, called it something different . . . *Rampage Day*. They knew entering this school was like traveling Dante's seven circles of hell. The bullying, the abuse, the shit food, and of course, the rats. Fucking fur demons that buttered the walls, keeping the heat in along with the disease.

"He's got freckles all over his face. I can't really tell, but something is wrong with his face. He looks about twelve, like us, and there is a big bandage on his left arm, covering his hand."

Archie pressed his forehead to the window. Dot rolled herself back, "Only one kid today, Wenty."

"That's odd," Wentworth exhaled. "Poor bastard. This is the first time only one child has been dropped off."

"Sister Carrie is out there waving her hands like a friggin' monkey," Dot said, laughing to herself.

"What do you mean?"

"She's talking to the driver and pointing at the boy. Something is wrong. I can't figure out what she's saying." Dot said, moving to her tiptoes to see from her chair out the high window. "She keeps pointing back toward the street."

"What's the kid doing?"

"Staring right at us," Dot said as she quickly ducked beneath the window pane. Wenty couldn't see, but the thought of it turned his arms prickly, like chicken skin.

Archie watched in waiting and lightly tapped the window, letting the vibrations rattle his skull.

After the confrontation, the new kid entered as Sister Carrie opened the large, creaky wooden door. Dot found it even more peculiar that the child had no bags, toys, or even a jacket. Most kids who come to Blackburn's at least have some personal belongings. Something to cling to that they claim as their own. But this kid came in empty-handed. With nothing but a broken body and a look of estrangement on his damaged face, he seemed to be seeing life for the first time. Dot noticed he did actually have something. It was protruding out of the top of his shirt pocket. Upon closer inspection, she realized it was a dandelion. Like a little cloud tethered to the boy's being, a white puff juxtaposed his leathered skin.

"Children," the nun said with her back stiff as she tried to regain composure after her interactions with the porter. "This is Francis. He's new here, and I'd like you to make sure he feels welcome."

The three kids stood motionless. Archie and Dot made eye contact after they realized those weren't freckles but burn scars. They made the boy's face look like fabric, as if his skin was hung from a clothing line. His flesh twirled toward the sky, leaving his black orb-like eyes to float like small planets. No brows, no eyelids or lashes, no lips. He looked as if God had forgotten how to make a face. Strands of fiery hair dangled lifelessly over tortured skin. Beneath where a nose should have been was a gaping hole that housed the smallest of teeth, like infant tombstones erected from hot pink gums.

Dot couldn't help herself and covered her mouth with her hands.

Wentworth was unintentionally facing the wrong way. He never was good at allowing sound to dictate his position or movements.

Fucking idiot, Dot thought to herself. It was just the right amount of sobriety she needed to remove the shock of meeting this burnt boy as she turned her friend around to face their new housemate.

"Francis," the nun started up again, "these are some of Blackburn's finest residents who've been with us the longest. Take Mr. Wentworth, for example. How long have you been here at Blackburn's?"

"As long as I can remember," Wentworth said with a prick of pride, pounding his cane into the stone floor.

"As you can see, Francis, Mr. Wentworth is encumbered with blindness. We have all sorts of children with his cursed situation."

"Cursed?" Wenty whispered to himself, gently touching his eyes.

"Here's another one of our special children. Dorothy, how about you? How long have you been with us now?"

"Since I was abandoned by my father here eight years, two months, and four days ago."

The nun suddenly felt like a warden at Dot's response. "Yes, yes, I remember the night well."

As the sister continued introducing the group, Francis's large black doll eyes never left Dot's face. She wasn't keen on one-on-one attention, especially from strangers, and instinctively scowled at the fire boy.

"And then there is Archibald," Sister Carrie said, her eyebrows crunching together. Archie smiled from ear to ear, just happy to be recognized by anyone. "Archibald, how long—oh, what's the point," Sister Carrie said, aborting her question. "Children, see that Francis finds his way around, and do fill him in on our little . . . *infestation.*"

"Absolutely, Sister Carrie," Dot said, raising her hand into a two-fingered salute. As Sister Carrie kept walking, Dot's hand morphed into a single middle finger, making Francis' head cock to the side like the hands of a clock. Nothing about him felt normal or even human-like, as Dot was hoping for some kind of giggle or inkling of youth at her immature gesture.

"Follow me," Dot said with visible discomfort as she waved at Francis. "So what the fuck happened to your face?"

Silence from the fire boy. Just his black holes for eyes, sucking in all of the unease of the moment like a drain. "What, you don't talk?" Dot asked, glancing back as she trudged through the dark hall, waiting, watching for any sign of life. "You can understand me at least, right?" Francis nodded, marinating in the moment he'd been waiting for.

Wenty wasn't far behind, tapping the floor with his cane, while Archie stayed and pulled dead flies from the windowsill and fed them to Puck, who was hidden within his overalls.

"Now listen, kid, the only thing you have to watch out for here is the food. It tastes like salty buttholes," Dot said.

Francis, again, was emotionless as he walked behind the roller girl.

"Don't forget to warn him about the nuns," Wenty interjected, smiling to himself.

"Right, the nuns are the real thing you have to watch out for. They're all crazy as headless ducks and ain't afraid to give you a swat if you disobey, especially Sister Carrie. You ever been spanked before in the name of God? It's enough to purge all of your sins."

"Oh, and the beds, Dot," Wenty added.

"Yes, the beds are the even realer thing you need to watch out for. They're hard as nails. Years ago, they used to have feathers, but now the soft part of each one has been, I don't know, smashed to dust. We think the rats have been taking them for their nests. Basically, we all sleep on old feather bone sticks."

"Tell him about the rats, Dot. Don't forget to

THE SISTERS

tell him about the rats," Wentworth intervened one final time.

Dot's wheelchair skidded to a halt. Even then, the children could hear the rats in the walls as if the architecture was filled with blood rushing through the school's veins. The chitter never stopped. It was enough to make a person crazy, a living static, a river of vermin pulsing all around them.

"Francis, listen," Dot said, poking him in the chest, "beware of the rats, you got that?! Don't be caught walking around without shoes on, and don't shit after dark, especially in the summer. And for God's sake, don't take *any* food to bed with you! Unless you want your food and maybe a finger to be gone by the morning."

Francis's face contorted like a circus performer. Dot could hear the skin stretch like old leather. And then she saw it, a smile. Leaving Dot even more bothered than before, the new kid's sinister face illuminated the hallway. His smile looked like a ventriloquist puppet coming to life. Before Dot could tell him to change his face—before she could do it for him—the breakfast bell rang loudly down the halls, allowing Archie to feel its reverberations beneath his feet. Soon, Archie's round little body came running through the group toward the mess hall.

Wenty dashed, and Dot followed, rolling away in a rush, leaving Francis alone in the hall to listen as the unseen rats scurried around him. Even though Francis's ears were nubs, he could still hear. He could still hear his purpose, like cathedral bells pulsating the songs of praise. Francis raised his hands to give a quick and quiet burst of applause, smashing his hand against his cast, whispering to himself, "*Ga ga ga.*"

IN FEBRUARY, as autumn turned increasingly nocturnal and leaves were replaced with powder, a ship came ashore from the sea carrying something within its hold, like a mother with a goblin in the womb, a tumor on the spine, a vespiary. Once docked, relieved sailors departed, but so did its other passengers: the rodents, each carrying a secret that would later be called the worst catastrophe in recorded history.

Living on each of the rodents were imperceptible black fleas, like black stars littered amongst brown cosmic fur known as the deadly bubonic plague that ravaged Europe, forever changing the social and economic fabric of humanity. The ship held the rats, the rats held the fleas, and the humans held the consequences. Small fleshy bubbles harboring bacteria began to bloom and pop in the humid parts of the body. The inguinal, vaginal, and scrotum areas harvested a viticulture of lumps and skin knobs, making the warm parts of one's anatomy like that of a cluster of yellowed grapes. These bubos bulged and squirted, spraying into the open air and traveling as quickly as rats could run, spreading to and infecting thousands, millions—killing, torturing, and stealing the lives of all who breathed. This ship, this doom-bringer, landed twenty-six point seven miles from Blackburn's Catholic School for the Orphan and Invalid, exactly fifteen days ago in the region of Hamelin.

"HEY, PIG TITS," Henry said, tapping his pewter tray next to the deaf boy.

Archie could tell that whatever Henry was saying wasn't good. Henry, not getting the rise he wanted out of Archie, slapped Archie's ass—hard. Archie swung in his direction, chin high and war ready. This exchange sent electricity to all of the children in the dining hall, and soon a buzz flickered.

"What the fuck, Henry?" Dot said, abandoning her spot in the cafeteria line, wheeling toward the commotion.

"Stay out of this, cripple. This is between me and Oinker here."

"God, it all makes so much sense now. It's no wonder your family abandoned you here at Blackburn."

"Dot, don't," Wenty interjected from the back of the line.

Henry's anger was stoked, and his curiosity peaked. "Oh yeah, rolling bitch? Why is that?" Henry said with a domineering smile, leaning down to grip the armrests of Dot's chair.

"Tell me, your siblings weren't dropped off with you, correct?" Dot said, scratching her chin. "Your parents handed *you* over, but not them . . . Odd," Dot added with such perfectly timed sarcasm, it felt like a song. Wenty never agreed with Dot's ambition, but he respected it.

Henry, in visible discomfort, pressed his iron fork firmly into Dot's thigh. "I don't think you want me to get mad."

Archie watched, his blood boiling. "It's okay, Archie," Dot said, using a downward motion with her hands to reinforce her words. She turned back and smiled at Henry's threat, "Well, just like your parents, it sounds like no one wants you at all, let alone mad."

"Shut the fuck up, you—" Before Henry could finish his roar, Archie threw his hot bowl of orphan-approved soup at the back of Henry's head, knocking him to the floor and splashing Dot with its searing remnants. Chunks of boiled carrot and cabbage were flung every which way as students ducked for cover with their trays and hands. Unfazed, Dot pulled the fork from her thigh like Arthur pulling the sword from the stone and shouted, "FOOD FIGHT!" She took one of the baked potatoes from the cafeteria line and threw it aimlessly at the other tables filled with children.

Archie joined in, smashing and smearing food against Henry's unconscious body. Wentworth couldn't contain himself any longer and exploded with rebellion, launching his food from his tray at those around him. Well, at least he thought so. Dot would never have the heart to tell him he was throwing food at the wall, not the other children. This caused quite a scene, as the food he threw ricocheted from his opponent—the brick wall—right back at him, fueling his efforts.

"Dorothy. Wentworth. Archibald," Sister Carrie shouted from the doorway. "What in God's name has gotten into you?!"

Amid the chaos, Dot realized it was only herself, Wenty, and Archie rebelling with food for ammo. Every other child sat and watched in shock and disgust, some hiding under tables, others cleaning food out of their clothing and hair.

"Sister Carrie, hang on. Henry—"

"Oh, shady day. Henry Broomfield, the child in front of you, is clearly unconscious."

"Yes, he was bullying Archie, so I—"

"Don't you dare," the nun thundered, her command reverberating through the arched stone ceilings.

Dot surrendered. No amount of excuses could rescue her.

"The scum of the earth, that is what you three are," the nun said. She tried to awaken Henry. "The three of you have additional assignments for the next month."

"Fuuuucckkkk me," Dot whispered to herself. "I already have assignments."

"How do three more months sound?"

"Dot, stop, please!" Wenty said with force behind her.

"Wentworth, report to the groundskeeper. Dorothy to the nursery ward, and Archie . . . Oh, what's the point." The nun said, giving up. "You're about as useful as climbing a tree to catch a fish, Archibald."

Archie, unsure of what she was saying and covered in breakfast, gave a smirk.

Sweet are the uses of adversity which,
like the toad, ugly and venomous,
wears yet a precious jewel in his head.

—William Shakespeare

"YOU'RE QUITE GOOD WITH BABIES, DOROTHY," the night mother said, handing Dot a warm blanket that was perched near the fireplace. The nursery ward was the warmest wing within the school, as the staff went to great lengths to avoid crying little ones. Peace and quiet was Blackburn's biblical mission, and anything that threatened that was met with wrath.

"I'm actually not that good with babies, but this one doesn't seem to think I'm a troll," Dot said, unlocking the makeshift baby cage.

"She's taken quite a liking to you these past few weeks," the night mother replied, conjuring the slightest smirk in one corner of her mouth as she reached in to seize the baby and hand her to Dot.

"Do you think she knows?" Dot asked, swaddling the child in her arms.

"Knows what?" the night mother asked, setting the crib key on the arm of Dot's chair.

"That we're both . . . you know?"

The night mother paused her morning rounds as she finally became aware of Dot's display of vulnerability. A rare event indeed, one that shouldn't go unnoticed. "Yes, Dorothy. I think Claire does know that you two both are . . . paralyzed."

Dot's eyes locked on the night mother. Finally, she broke her gaze and looked down at the broken baby in her lap. She gingerly tucked its blonde hair behind its ears, the hair soft as an angel's. "I promise I won't let anything happen to you," she whispered.

"That's quite a promise," the night mother said, overhearing Dot's vow.

Startled at the night mother's inordinate hearing skills for being such an old crooner, Dot replied, "Someone has to look out for her. God knows no one did for me."

"What makes you think that, Dorothy?"

Dot shrugged, allowing her rebellious spirit another minute of strength. "Will she get a small chair like I had?" Dot asked, changing the subject.

"Not just *like* yours, your exact one."

"Blackburn's still has it?"

"Of course! Infant invalid chairs are a pretty penny. You bet your bottom we kept it."

"Hopefully you grease it up for Claire before you give it to her. There were many times it'd lock up on me, making me tardy," Dot said with a chuckle.

"It feels like a lifetime before Claire will need that, but that's what I said about you, and look at you now. You're a young lady now. I see you hanging around those boys," the night mother said with a wink.

"Wenty and Archie?"

"Yes, those two. You three are like a tricycle. Take a wheel away, and you all become wobbly."

"We're friends, that's all."

"Is it now? Even with Wentworth?" the night mother said with a grin. "Don't think I don't notice the way you act around each other."

"Jesus Christ," Dot said sharply.

"Watch it, young lady. I may be more liberal than the rest here, but I'm still a practicing Christian."

Dot gave a small squeeze to the slumbering baby. "Sorry, I'm late for class," Dot said, giving Claire a goodbye kiss on her forehead and gently handing her to the night mother. "Alright, I'll see you tomorrow," Dot whispered.

"Scoot! Scoot! Hurry!" The night mother announced, shooing the girl away. "Oh wait, one more thing," the night mother reached into her apron and pulled a small piece of chocolate wrapped in cloth. "I bought this at the store in town. I thought you'd like a small treat for how much you've been helping out around here."

"You're the fucking best," Dot said, wrapping her arms around the night mother.

"Stop that. What were some of those supplementary words I shared with you?" she scolded but still reciprocated the hug.

"Oh right, sorry. You're the *frinkliest*?" Dot said with a smile.

As Dot rolled herself into the hall, the night mother stayed and nestled Claire in her crib. The heavenly cooing of babies and the night mother's gentle lullabies filled the air, drowning out the ever-present sounds within the walls. The sounds of little nightmares scraping and twitching just beyond the stones, drilling and expanding their world among the school grounds, unbeknownst to its primary inhabitants.

•   •   •

"Ask, and it will be given to you; seek, and you will find; knock, and the door will be opened to you," the sister said, placing her small black bible on the school desk. "Children, what do these words mean to you?"

Like so many other students forced to sit in a classroom on a sunny day, the class stared blankly at the teacher, their eyes glazed and their minds vacant. Children tapped their fingers against the cold desks. Biblical tapestry and legends of the great saints lined the classroom walls. Candles were lit in the corners, holding the nuns' prayers and marking the walls above them in black soot.

"Well, go on. Don't be afraid to get it wrong. This is a discussion, not a test," the nun exhorted.

Sarah, the one with big gums in the back, took the sister's bait. "It means God the Father will only give to those who ask for it."

Dot rolled in. There was no point being quiet—everyone could hear her chair as it rumbled across the stone floor. She gave an audible snort of protest upon hearing Sarah's answer as she placed her arms on the cold desk.

"Something you'd like to contribute, Ms. Tardy?" Sister Teresa added snarkily.

"No, not today," Dot said, a bit out of breath. "Sorry I'm late. I was helping in the nursery."

"Well, as your consequence for being late, tell us *your* opinion."

Dot looked around the room. Half of the children were awake; the other half was uninterested. "Um . . ."

"'Um' is not a response," the teacher scolded.

"To be honest—"

"What else would you be in a house consecrated to the Lord?"

"Well, I've been knocking on God's door for years, and I got news for you. He ain't home." Three desks over, Wentworth gave his usual supportive chuckle.

"So, you believe that God is nonexistent just because you haven't gotten what you wanted?"

"I've learned that when you have legs like mine, a philosophy of materialism rings more true than ever."

"That is quite a sentence for a young girl," the nun said, a bit dumbfounded.

"I don't mean any offense. It's just that—"

"No offense taken," the nun interrupted, leaning back on her large wooden desk. "But I'm curious about where your—how did you say it?—*philosophy of materialism*, yes, that's it. Where will this materialism take you?"

Dot shifted her weight in her chair, preparing for a rebuttal, "What do you mean?"

The nun removed a ruler from a small cistern on her desk, tapping it against her palm. "No doubt you've been reading Dr. Franklin Berlinksky's book in the library on methodological naturalism, but did you read enough to truly change your logic? Or just enough to add epistemological hurdles to your opponents?" The sister was throwing her sesquipedalian tail around in hopes of whipping some sense into the girl who couldn't walk.

"I just think if there was a loving God, *as you all believe* . . . then he should do loving things." An audible rumbling sparked among the other classmates. "Exhibit A," she said, gesturing toward her lower half. "Taking a girl's legs and making them work again. So as long as I don't have legs to run with, I'm a materialist."

"That makes sense, Dorothy," the nun replied, moving closer. "My only concern is this: either a deity is a material object or he is not. If God is, then he must be a thing; if he is not, then materialism cannot be true."

Dot was at a loss for words, feeling the blank spaces in her mind for a comeback.

"If God is just one of those things, what is his interest or purpose? And if materialism is false, why are we even bothering to engage in this topic in the first place?" the nun tapped Dot's desk with her ruler. "My conclusion then is that you're not a materialist. You're too smart for that. I think you do believe in God. You need him. You want him."

"I want him?"

"Well . . ." the nun adjusted her thought, "he's all you have. What other options do you have other than a god?"

Dot's gaze drifted toward the window, where she watched snowflakes fall from the heavens. To her, it solidified her point, that heaven is a cold-hearted place. Or at least she thought. As the other children dreamed of a place beyond, a place flooded with golden streets, roasted meat, and healthy bodies, Dot dreamed of now. Heaven was there, she couldn't deny that, but unless God proved himself here, heaven was no place she wanted to be.

Sister Teresa gave a slight smile to the girl who couldn't walk and walked back to her own desk, her black robe swishing with each step.

Dot never liked nuns. She viewed them more as living ghosts than ministers. The way they'd float from room to room, only a small portion of their face shining from the storm cloud of their dressing. *Ghosts with purpose*, but maybe that's why she hated them. Even as ghosts they had something to live for.

The loud church bell rang from the crow's nest of the school as children shot up like weasels from their holes and raced toward their next tutorship.

"The lord loves you as you are," Sister Teresa said to Dot as she made her way to the door.

Dot gave an uncomfortable nod to the nun and grabbed Wenty's arm on her way out. "I need a fucking smoke. *Purgatory?*"

BEHIND THE GARDENER'S SHED, hidden from the school's windows, was their spot. They felt like settlers discovering an untouched piece of land, unseen by the rest of the world—a place they could call their own. Dot coined it "Purgatory," as it felt like a bosom between heaven and hell. A place brimming with smoke from their tomato bowl pipes and hot breath mingling with the icy cold air.

The three of them decided to skip their next class, as it was nicer outside with the snow and cold sunshine. The icy wind was warmer than Sister Teresa's algebraic theory lectures. They bundled up and made their way to the only place they felt themselves.

"God, Sister Teresa, what a fucktrumpet," Dot said, as frosty as the ice beneath their feet.

"Dot, dude, give them a break," Wenty said, handing the matchbox to the lame girl.

"What's with you?"

"You're just always shitting on them. Blackburn's. God. Be careful is all I'm saying."

"Be careful? Of what, Wenty?" Dot said, pulling out a match.

"I mean, I don't know. I'm just trying to make the best of it and not upset anyone."

"Yeah, you're coping with this hellhole, and I am too. I just do it through savage takedowns and sardonic smiles!" Dot said, raising her hand to Archie for a slap. Archie wasn't paying attention and gave her one out of routine.

"Whatever. Don't shit on God, dude," Wenty said, growing annoyed. "You're afraid of him anyways."

"An all-loving, invisible, tucked-away-in-heaven God sure doesn't sound like something I'd be afraid of," Dot said, exhaling her tobacco through a laugh.

"Woe is you, if every prayer gets answered."

"What?" Dot asked.

"It's something Sister Teresa said. Woe to you if every prayer gets answered."

"Please don't tell me you're a theologian now?" Dot mocked, passing Archie the pipe.

Wenty exhaled. "I don't know, I like bible stuff. I like the stories."

"Jesus Christ, Wenty."

"Yeah, him too," Wenty laughed back, trying to diffuse the moment. "I just think what she was saying makes a lot of sense."

"No, it doesn't."

"To make God do something would make you God, wouldn't it?"

Dot was silent. The theology landed heavily in her lap, along with a dose of frustration with Wentworth. She didn't like to be criticized. Especially when he was right.

"Imagine, Dot, that everything you tell him to do, he does. You'd be God. I'd be God. Archie would be God. Because God is God and ought to be God. Therefore, it's right for God to be God and right for you *not* to be God," Wenty said, head tilted up toward the sky as he spoke, trying to make sense of his own words.

"What's your point?" Dot snapped back, inhaling the tobacco, getting distracted as Archie wrote something on his chalkboard.

THE BOY WHO COULDN'T SEE

"I don't know . . . That God knows what is good for me better than I do? More than you do?"

"So my legs, they're all part of his good plan?"

"I didn't say that, nor do I believe that," Wenty said, changing his tone. They felt the winter air enter their emotions. "Maybe there is a plan."

"Fuck off, Wentworth," Dot whispered, half kidding and half serious.

"GrAce iS the hArsh wiNd wiCh bloWS leaVes frUm trees, withOUt it, DeR wOuLd nOt be sPRrinG."

Was scrawled upon Archibald's chalkboard dangling from his neck.

Dot stared at the words. "I understand, Archie. Thank you." Archie read her lips and smiled at her. Dot snuck Wenty a quick middle finger he'd never see and turned to tamp her pipe out when she noticed it. Beneath their feet, birthed from the ice before their very eyes, they witnessed something no one had ever seen. A singular blossom of a dandelion, a slow-motion floret coming into the universe at an unnatural speed.

"SISTER CARRIE, DO YOU HAVE A MINUTE?" Father Gregory asked as the nun floated by his study door.

"Certainly, Father."

"Yesterday's Ramp Day . . ."

"Yes, I know. I was just as surprised as you were."

"No, I don't think you were. I told you specifically that we are taking no more new students until our vermin problem has been eradicated. Sister Margaret spoke to the mayor, correct?"

"She did. She felt the meeting was futile, to say the least."

"How is that possible?"

"I didn't authorize this, but when I spoke to the driver he told me someone had paid good money to bring this child to Blackburn's."

"Curious."

"Deeply so."

"Where is the paperwork for the burned boy?"

"Well," Sister Carrie said, bringing her hand to her throat, "this deepens the mystery. The driver told me it was sent over before his arrival, but I found no such documents."

"Did you ask the boy where he came from? Who sent him?"

"I did."

"And?"

"Well, I'd rather not say."

"Excuse me?" the father asked with growing annoyance.

"I just mean, I found it rather upsetting."

"Go on," the priest said, intrigued.

"Well, I asked him where he's from, and he smiled. Then I asked him who sent him, and he said . . ." The nun touched her throat, coaxing the words out. "All of hell and its wonderful torments brought him here. Then he stuck his tongue in and out of his mouth like a snake."

The priest smiled, amused at the boy's ego. Blackburn's had seen countless personalities come through its doors over the years. Even the most broken child had something to prove. They must do something to stand out among their peers. To feel valuable or needed.

Father Gregory stroked the back of his neck and reached for his tobacco and loose-leaf paper. He rolled his cigarette skillfully and stuck it in his mouth like a feather in a cap. "I have zero paperwork, and without it we can't register the boy. If we can't register the boy, then we can't foster the boy, and if we can't foster the boy . . ."

"We don't get funding, I understand."

"Exactly, Sister."

"What would you like me to do? How can I help?"

"Well, it's no major rush because, well, let's be honest, there isn't a high demand for severely burned children with demon-like attitudes," the father said, smirking with his eyes. Sister Carrie squirmed in her chair.

"Speak with him and find out who *really* sent him here, who paid for his transportation, and who has his paperwork, and Chrissake get me his last name."

"Yes, Father."

"Oh, and do me one more favor," the priest said, smashing his cigarette into his brass ashtray. "Tell young Dorothy to find me as soon as possible."

Sister Carrie paused as she stood up, like a living photograph, allowing Father Gregory to see her discomfort with his command. "It's quite late. Perhaps another time you can be with Dorothy?"

"Bring me the girl."

The sister stood in place, wanting to say more but fearing retribution.

"That'll be all, Sister Carrie," the father said, rolling up his sleeves.

As the other children were getting ready for bed, Dot stayed in her chair. Waiting. Every Tuesday and Thursday before bed, the priest would beckon the lame girl. Wenty lay there listening to her wheels glide back and forth nervously, knowing she'd be back in a couple of hours, smaller than when she left. Wenty couldn't prove it, but he felt that every time she did her "lessons," as Father Gregory called them, she returned with less than before she went. It was as if she was made of ice, slowly melting. If Wenty

PRIEST

had eyes, *or balls*, he'd crash open the door to Father Gregory's study and rescue Dot from whatever black magic was going on in there. He tried to not allow his thoughts to wander too far.

"Dot," Sister Carrie whispered from the door. "Father Gregory has need of you."

Wenty listened to her reluctant wheels take her into hell. As the door closed, Wentworth punched his chest repeatedly, beating his fearful heart before he rolled over to his own black nightmares, the only place he could see, the only place that felt like home. But before he could pull the blanket over his head, he felt the presence of something or someone beside his bed. Wenty couldn't feel his own eyes, but he could feel others'. A blackness at the end of his bed, a living gargoyle perched and waiting. The suffocation was enough to end the blind boy. "Archie?" he said in a whisper to the deaf boy, then kicking himself as he remembered.

"You say something, Wentworth?" Giggy asked from the corner of the large room.

"No, you fat, friggin' baby-dick! Fart yourself back to sleep!" Wenty whispered-shouted at the kid.

But the feeling didn't evaporate as Wentworth lay still, waiting to hear if something was watching him. He could still feel it.

Wenty gave it another go. "Simon? Sarah? That you?" Wenty's senses came alive, his skin tingled, and his breath deepened as he caught a whiff of something sour nearby. The sound of a being was steady at the foot of Wenty's bed. "This isn't funny. I want to go to sleep. Leave me the fuck alone!" Wenty said, reaching for his cane. He sat up, waving it slowly like a senseless magician in the dark. Side to side, up and down, nothing. Then as he brought it toward the end of his bed, it collided with something. *Someone.*

His heart froze mid-beat at the thought of it. "Who's there?" Wenty aimed at the perp with his cane, fear prickling his skin like ice. No response, just steady breaths, like a sleeping giant. The feeling of being watched, combined with the inability to watch back, was beginning to drown the boy.

"I warned you," Wenty said and swung his cane from right to left, bringing it hard on the person standing at the edge of his bed. The sound was sharp, congratulating Wenty's aim, but was met with no movement or jerk, not even a gasp of pain, inviting a horrible sense of fright to the unseeing boy.

Wenty had a thought so horrible, his lips could barely push it out, "Francis?" And just like that, he heard the soft and quick footsteps of the presence scurry and wander off as Dot opened the door and rolled into the bunk room.

"What are you still doing up?" Dot whispered.

That was fast, Wenty thought to himself.

Wenty knew that if Dot didn't see anything or anyone there, it'd be pointless to bring it up. Plus, he knew better than anyone that if he were to mention it, Dot would have stuck a spoon in Francis's forehead before that fire boy had a chance to say "sloppynuts."

"Waiting for you," he said, lying. "Your lesson this time seemed rather quick."

"I told him I wasn't feeling well and he shooed me off like a fly."

"You're not feeling well?" Wenty asked concernedly.

"Girl stuff, dude."

"Oh, right," Wenty whispered, pretending to know about female anatomy.

"When will you tell me what happens with Father Gregory?"

"Never. Ain't none of your business."

"We're friends, aren't we?"

"The best of!"

"Then isn't it my business?"

"It's best if you don't know."

"Fine. Fuck it, I don't care."

"Wenty, geez, we're not married. Take it easy," Dot said before she checked on Archie like she did every night.

"Whatever," Wenty croaked back, removing the dirty wrap from his eyes.

"Relax, hubby, or you'll wake our wittle boy," Dot said, laughing to herself.

"Go get a fork and eat my hole, wifey," Wenty snapped back, still mad but unable to resist joining in. At his bedside, Dot watched the deaf boy roll over beneath his blanket. She could see he was playing with his pet. She listened to his mumbled and failed words, smiling at his childlike innocence as she put herself to bed.

Beneath the scratchy blanket, Archie felt Puck's soft purr beneath his fingers. Between pets, Archie would lean in for a kiss, allowing Puck to lick his nose and lips. He reminded himself that no matter what Wenty or others may think of rats or mice, he loved them like Jehovah loves Cain. He loved them the way he wished to be loved and wanted.

Archie grabbed his flashlight and a copy of *Macbeth* and opened it to its dog-eared page. He always craved adventure or the opportunity to be heroic like Shakespeare's mighty men. He told his spirit he just needed a chance. He needed a dragon outside the city or a damsel in distress. Readying his heart for the day he too could be a hero. But, unbeknownst to Archie, a woman in need of a hero unleashed a terrifying scream just beyond their bedroom door.

THE SHRIEK SHOOK THE DUST OFF the brick walls—
the type of scream that hurts to hear.

Dot immediately shot up, dragging her limp
body back to her chair. Wentworth, a bed down
from her, patted for his cane frantically as Archie
slept. The other misfit children began to rise from
their sleep like zombies as the screaming turned into
guttural moaning. Giggy, of course, was the first to
speak. "What's happening?" he mumbled through
fish lips.

"Quiet, you horse ass!" Dot yelled at him in a
whisper, lighting a candle near her bed to illuminate
the room. The children could hear the pastors,
nuns, and staff rumble down the hallway toward the
horrifying scream.

"It sounds like a teacher is screaming," Wentworth whispered to Dot. "Why would a teacher be
screaming like that?"

Dot peeked back, glancing at Archie still under his blanket with a light, unaware and innocent. Then as she scanned the room, noting child after child leaving their cotton coffins, she saw Francis with the blanket wrapped around his head like a hood, facing her. Her heart stopped as she saw that same crooked smile from earlier in the hallway.

It was a moment of great polarization as the screams resounded through the school, and Francis smiled at the sound of it. Dot quickly removed Francis from her thoughts as she opened the door slightly, peering into the darkened hallway. "I don't see anything."

"Me neither," Wenty said, making Dot snort in laughter.

"You fucking idiot, that was funny," Dot said with a smile, punching him in the arm. Then, with heroic bravery, Dot rolled into the hallway and moved toward the commotion. "Come on, Wenty."

"I can't . . . I'm afraid."

"Fine, stay here like a bitch."

Dot was always moving toward the action. Like a buzzard circling death, her magnetic wings brought her to whatever the danger was. She could hear screaming coming from the infant hall of the school and sped her chair there as quickly as she could. There were multiple doors into the nursery from the hallway, and she made her way to the furthest one to avoid any detection.

The other infants in the wing had all been awakened by the scream, and they too joined in. Dot's skin crawled as a chorus of baby screeches concerted the room, filling it like a gas, making her hide her ears from the noise. From where she was in the shadows, she could see the teachers and staff hovering over the crib in the middle of the room. Each one with bulging eyes and hands over their mouths in shock. Dot couldn't hear what they were saying over the screams, but she saw Sister Margaret gesture to grab something, and they filed out of there like train cars, allowing Dot to roll closer to the scene.

As brave as she was, at that moment she wished she had Archie's deaf ears and Wentworth's blind eyes. She wished she had stayed in bed or that her curious spirit wasn't as strong as it was. Because what she witnessed that night was enough to haunt a thousand dreams. Her dinner soon ejected itself from her stomach and made a mess of her paralyzed legs.

"Oh God . . . Claire," she whispered through the vomit.

The rats, in fact, who swarmed by thousands in the carcass of the elephant, and who were the living black spots which we have already mentioned, had been held in awe by the flame of the candle, so long as it had been lighted; but as soon as the cavern, which was the same as their city, had returned to darkness, scenting what the good story-teller Perrault calls "fresh meat."

—**Victor Hugo**

STEAM LIFTED OFF DOT'S PINK CHEEKS as hot tears streamed from reddened eyes. No noise except for the occasional sniffle came from the girl. Her eyes were locked in place, staring at nothing but seeing everything. The fire cherry went out within the bowl she had lit, a symbol of a fire going out in the lame girl.

"What did you see last night?" Wenty asked. "We want to help, but you have to let us in."

"Don't ask me to describe it to you. I won't," Dot turned her wheelchair toward the northern snowy hills.

Archie was never good at tamping his tobacco, so his pipe usually fizzled out before the others, leaving him to eat snow or stare at the others' lips awkwardly. Dot could see he was pulling something billowy and white from the snow. He examined it as she examined him. She always found herself watching Archibald, the way geese watch goslings. These emotions competed with the loss of another gosling.

"Listen," Dot said as she wiped her eyes and turned her chair back to face them. "We need to talk." The tone of her command forced the boys to realize this was more than friends getting together. "Give me your chalkboard, Archie," she said, pointing at the board. Archie dropped whatever he was fiddling with and did as he was told.

"We need to make a pact. A . . . a promise that no matter what happens in the next few days we'll be there for each other," she said, frantically spelling the word "PROMISE" on Archie's chalkboard.

"Jesus, Dot, what happened last night?" Wenty asked, itching the scars beneath his eye bandage.

"Wentworth, it was the worst thing I've ever seen."

"Dot, tell us what's going on!"

"It's Claire, god dammit!"

Silence fell. It was such deep silence that Wenty thought he could hear the falling snow.

"They ate her," Dot said, but just barely. Her

strength failed, and the gates that held back her courage fell open.

"I thought you told me that the nursery cribs have cages?" Wenty asked, relighting his pipe.

"They do."

"So what the fuck?" Wenty responded.

Dot opened her hand, exposing crib cage keys. Archie peered into her palm like a hungry animal. "I forgot to give the key back to the night mother," Dot said, devastated. "Oh my god," she whispered again, reliving the thought.

"It was an accident, Dot," the blind boy said. "And now it's a secret." Wenty had never heard Dot cry, let alone moan. His cold hand grabbed Dot's and Archie's. No words were said, but they didn't need to be.

Dot wiped her tears with her sleeve and breathed in deeply. "It happened here, in our home, the place we live. We have no one to protect us, and I'm scared. I want us to make a blood pact here and now that no matter what, we will fight for each other." Dot frantically erased the chalkboard and wrote the words "fight for each other" on the board. Archie nodded, but Wenty's nerves got the better of him. Perhaps it was because he couldn't see and had no way to gauge the situation, forcing him to question everything and everyone.

"We are all we have," she added, "and this is my dumb attempt to try and make sure that doesn't change."

Wenty could hear it now, the genuineness blossoming from her words. He took the iron pipe tamper from his pocket and cut a canyon into his palm. Like an artist, he painted the white snow crimson. Archie reached over and took the tamper, making his own skin come apart. Dot began to tear up at the realization that she had family, warming the cold moment. She too cut her palm on the sharp edge of her wheelchair, and each of them brought their hands together, blood dancing, a marriage in its own way. The hot blood caused them to smile and giggle, unaware this would be the last time they were happy together.

● ● ●

"The baby was eaten alive. It would have been entirely eaten to its bones if the night mother hadn't been doing her evening rounds. Searching for the occasional rebel or fornicating teenager, she patrolled room to room, entering with a lantern and sharp eye, but upon entering the nursery she heard a sound. A sound that shouldn't be associated with children. Crunches and innocent muffles cut through the quiet room.

"As the night mother went from crib to crib, she finally found the cause. It was not just a baby but rather an infant (as it was known for decades to come). The infant writhed beneath its blanket, the way a body moves when it's no longer within its reality, like an out-of-water cephalopod or beheaded snake.

"The metamorphosis took place, from child to meal, flesh to shit. The infant could not scream— rats had taken its tongue and burrowed their way through the tiny skull's soft skin opening, which lay at the top of her head like a wishing well. The child was stripped of skin, just muscle and tissue, as if the baby had been turned inside out. Or fileted like a hunter's catch. Its bright blue eyes were the only cooling color in the sludge of purple that soaked the polka-dot sheets.

"No human with any conscience or human morality could witness the scene and not harrowed in pain. After seeing a sight that would change the direction of anyone's entire life, our night mother swiftly and permanently removed herself from the school, nunship, and faith entirely. To her, there could be no possible god, only the devil."

"Jesus Christ, I don't know what to say, or—" the mayor said through limp words. His eyes were pink from the shock of it all. It was the first genuine emotion the nun had seen from the reptile that was the mayor.

"This could have been avoided, don't you think?" Sister Margaret asked sharply, setting the canvas sack on his desk.

"I promise to pay for the extermination," the mayor said, visibly uncomfortable. He turned his chair around to face the wall—anything to avoid Sister Margaret's eyes. "But you must promise the staff at Blackburn's to keep this matter hidden from the public. The entire school would be shut down, I would lose the election, and you'd be out of a job, Sister."

Sister Margaret couldn't see the mayor's face but

could hear the sincerity in his voice. She was good at that. *A spiritual gift*, she thought. Discernment of spirits was something she prided herself on, and in this moment the mayor possessed a spirit of mercy. This allowed Sister Margaret to see the skinless baby as she saw the incarnate baby of Christ. A life taken so more can be spared. A ransom. From death shall come life. "By the end of this week, I expect to not see any rats within my school."

And with that, the door closed, leaving the mayor with a dead infant on his desk.

AS CHAPEL WAS WRAPPING UP at the other end of the school, the fire boy roamed the halls of Blackburn freely. Education was not his purpose here. He rubbed one exposed hand down the wall of the long corridor, the way one might touch an unbroken horse, petting its wild, velvet skin with both trepidation and reverence. He did his best to ignore the other hand's muffled screams from within its cast-enveloped prison.

Slowly, he let his eyes assess the school's magnificence. Never had he been in such a spiritual place. His black eyes glistened as they did when he first met God. Wanting to touch the flying buttresses and tall arches, he reached his hands out, aligning them to his eyes as he pretended to stroke every stone curve. It was as if he had an invisible paintbrush in his hand, stroking, conducting, casting spells. He marveled at the ornamental columns, realizing that the design brought his attention toward the gods.

He wondered as he took in the ornate, stained glass that kissed the walls, illuminating their stories of saints and martyrs, if stained glass might ever be crafted in memoriam of his own daring adventure, of what he was about to do at this school. He could see the orange glass from the harvest moon color the shafts of morning light onto the attentive congregation. He liked that; he could feel it in his body.

Other children ran beside him as the lunch bells banged their song, pulling Francis back from his rapture. They went one way and Francis another, the way it's always been. Despite having no nose, the holes in his face could smell the boiled meat, onions, and leeks coming from the kitchen, but Francis wasn't hungry. Not for food. He was thirsty. He had an insatiable thirst.

Won't mother be so happy, he thought.

He stopped at the abandoned nursery, peering in as the hallway's rainbow-colored light silhouetted him. The stench of death fogged the room. He sniffed hard, filling his gray lungs with the smell. Francis slowly moved toward the crib, the only crib with a black stained mattress in a sea of white baby beds. His large, glassy eyes were wet with anticipation, and his tongue frantically licked the air like a serpent as he gave a small explosion of applause.

Stealthily, he looked for any sign of the infant. A trail, a note, a clue. But before he could seize the moment, he heard two intruders enter the other end of the hall, forcing Francis to quickly abandon his quest and retreat to the shadows, his desired spot. There, he heard their secret conversation. The exact secret he wanted to know: the whereabouts of the dead infant. He finally discovered it thanks to the nuns' soft words as they quickly packed their boxes with blankets, not wanting to linger in the room any longer than they had to.

Satisfaction filled him as he quietly emerged from his hiding place and crawled into the coffin crib.

There he could see a filthy tag embroidered on the mattress with the infant's name inscribed, yarn smeared with blood. *Claire.*

His heart was pounding like a machine. Gingerly, he removed the sheet from its hard mattress and folded it neatly under his arm. Before returning to the shadows, he took a moment to lie his head against the blood-red-turned-black crib. Tucked in tightly, he imagined what it was like to be consumed by rats and giggled at the thought, only to be distracted by the sound of a wheelchair whizzing by the nursery toward the dining hall. He watched Dot avoid looking into the room before making silent but rapid applause from the crib. She rolled by with the blind and deaf boys staggering behind her.

Goosey, goosey, gander, whither dost thou wander? he thought to himself.

"ʀ A ᴛ s Kᴀɴ ɴᴇᴠᴇʀ sᴛOP ᴄʜUWIɴG," Archie scribbled on his chalkboard at lunch. His eyes boiled with happiness as he crumbled hard crackers in his hands and sprinkled them in the front pocket of his overalls for Puck. He watched as Puck's jaw moved in a machine-like rhythm. "Not now, Archie," Wenty said with exhaustion, filling his hole with taters.

Dot threw her fork down onto her pewter plate and rolled away from the table. Her appetite had vanished after what she had seen. Archie wiped the chalkboard to write new facts about rats. "Tey kepP chUwin, to stop dAr teef from grwn."

"That's enough, Archie!" Dot said, slamming her fists on the table. She'd had enough. Reaching for his chalkboard and wiping it clean once more, she wrote the words that would destroy the deaf boy.

"exterminator coming 4 rats"

She faced the chalkboard at Archie as if it were a mirror. He saw the words, but he barely comprehended them. Archie took the chalkboard, his only communication channel, and gazed back at Dot with a mixture of disbelief and broken disposition. Dot could see the message wasn't landing and tried again.

"All. Rats Will. Die!" she spoke out loud while writing.

"Jesus, Dot," Wenty grumbled.

"What, Wenty? This is what you wanted, isn't it?"

"Dot, I don't like rats, but I do like Archie. Take it easy."

Archie watched them bicker like seabirds as his grip on the chalkboard tightened. The only sound that could stop Dot and Wenty from their quarrel was the snap of Archie's broken board.

Dot could see that she'd finally gotten through to him, and she instantly regretted it.

"I'm sorry," she mouthed, returning to her motherly ways. Archie shot up from his seat and stormed out of the dining hall, his red eyes never leaving Dot's.

"Archie, are you going to finish your taters? I'm still hungry," Wentworth asked, unaware Archie was gone.

"Holy fuck, I need new friends," Dot said, rubbing her eyes.

• • •

The mayor ran the quill between his fingers, allowing it to tangle like an executioner's noose. He checked the ledger meticulously, crossing and scratching away at the figures. Frustrated, he flicked the quill onto the floor. "These are way too goddamn expensive!" he cried. "Rosemary, how many more local exterminators do we have?" he shouted, lighting his fifth pipe of the morning.

"None, sir. That's it."

"That can't be . . . What about hunters or trappers? Taxidermists, for Christsake? I pay you to think, don't I?"

Rosemary cleared her throat, swallowing her rebuttal. "I'll check on that now, but it''s slim pickings with our *lack of resources*," Rosemary said, allowing her last few words to be as respectful as possible while still remaining truthful.

The mayor smiled at her tone, the way a madman does at his victim when provoked. "Don't do this, Rosemary. Not today," the mayor said, tamping the cherry gently. "Do me a favor, though, and call Blackburn's. Tell them we found someone, and they'll be there this weekend."

Rosemary stood from her chair, allowing her notepad to fall by her waist. "Let me get this straight. You want me to call God's school full of disregarded children, nuns, and priests and lie to them that their monstrous rat invasion will be handled this week even though we have zero prospects?"

The mayor stood from his desk, staring at his new secretary. He reminded himself she hadn't learned his "rules" for how he liked women to behave. "We'll find someone by then," he said through sharp teeth, "we're just instilling confidence so she doesn't go public."

"And if we don't find someone?"

"Then we'll handle this in a different way. A different kind of extermination."

His eyes met the calendar that hung beyond Rosemary's shoulders, containing the big red word

"ELECTION" scrawled across the second Tuesday of the month.

Rosemary watched curiously and with fear, unsure of the lengths the mayor would go to. The internal battle she faced forced her to leave his office. The mayor watched her exit as he let his mind drift from dominating the vote to dominating his secretary. The mayor needed a few pieces of kindling to ignite his imagination, and Rosemary's skirt was enough to spark it. The mayor bit his lip, drank from his glass, and grinned.

● ● ●

"Here, children," Sister Margaret came by in a flurry as she handed each of the children a small bottle. "See to it that Wentworth gets his too, won't you, Dorothy? Where's Archibald? Isn't he normally with you two, like the three monkeys you kids are?"

Dot's eyes were still fixated on Archie's empty seat.

"Dorothy, are you listening?"

"What? Oh, yes, yes, what is this stuff?" Dot asked.

"Peppermint oil. Apparently rats hate the damn stuff. Rub it on your skin, your sheets . . . Hell, rub it on your soul. It's our last attempt to keep them at bay until the exterminator comes this weekend. We just got the call from the mayor's office."

Dot offered a tiny nod of agreement with even less enthusiasm.

"Dorothy, I'll also need you to help us with the babies like you do. They too will need this rubbed on them and their diapers."

"So we don't have another dead one?" Dot watched as the nun's eyes grew.

"How do you know about that?"

"Everyone knows. Our night mother wasn't exactly quiet when she discovered poor Clarie," Dot said, poking her jiggly food playfully. "Do you think it's about time the school leadership protects and informs their students? We're not animals, you know. We deserve to know the happenings in our home."

Sister Margaret's wide eyes became slits.

"I mean, that's the job of any school, isn't it? To inform? I'd hate to have to educate the other students myself," Dot said, motioning around the dining hall.

"What are you getting on about? Do you know what you're doing with these threats?"

"I do."

"And your aim is?"

"The same as it's always been."

The nun rubbed her eyes, frustration showing on her face. "You know we can't do that. There is no one looking to adopt invalids."

"Why won't you let me meet any of them?" Dot asked, letting her emotions get the best of her. But she didn't care anymore. Her emotions were her weapon. "If I could just meet a mother or father, I'm sure—"

"That's quite enough!" the nun barked.

The moment was quiet other than Wenty's tater chewing. "Sister . . ." Dot intervened with one last attempt.

"What do you want, child?"

"Where is the night mother?"

"Sister Florence?"

Dot nodded.

"She, um . . ." the nun searched for the words,

but Dot could see none accepted the invitation. "She has left us. For good. Even the sisterhood."

Dot's eyes left the nun's and cascaded down to the floor, just as her countenance did. Her spirit shriveled within her, a dying fetus in the womb. But as quickly as her show of vulnerability came, it went. Dot stiffened her spine and squeezed her thoughts back, not allowing a single tear to break.

"I am sorry about that, Dorothy. I know you two have been close for many years. But know this—" But before the sister could finish her thought, another scream erupted from the boys' bathroom.

As Dot grasped the situation, her heart settled into the realization that her home was quickly becoming an inferno.

ARCHIE RAN INTO THE COMMUNITY BATHROOM, wiping the tears from his eyes. Archie was never good at confrontation or emotions in general. Not that he didn't feel them or think they were for a weaker mind, but because he felt too much of them. They forced him to listen to voices he didn't want to hear. Bellowing voices from the fire that burned in his chest.

Archie learned early on that being deaf didn't mean you couldn't listen. It meant you were compelled to hear every spark of agony your mind could think of. Being deaf to the outside world opens new internal worlds. Worlds that were never meant to be explored. When outside noise cannot enter, the mind will make its own—an endless torture that can't be silenced.

But, for the deaf boy, it wasn't all terrors and torture. Happiness was his responsibility. He chose to entertain or indulge without the outside knowing. As if everything within his skull were his and his alone. Archie's mind went to Shakespeare's words, "To unpathed waters, undreamed shores." The boy who could not hear shook his fists, his face in a screaming position but without sound. Soon, blood leaked out the sides of his clenched hands, inducing his own stigmata. With his sleeve, he aggressively rubbed his eyes, trying to make them go back from pink to white. If he rubbed hard enough, he could wipe away what Dot said. For Archie, no one was closer to him than Puck.

"Well, if it isn't my old pal, Archi-bald-head," Henry said as he made sure the door behind him shut tightly.

Archie could feel his presence, a growing mist. His eyes darted like wasps between Henry and the door he was guarding. The deaf boy's heart was beating loud enough that even he thought he could hear it. Henry got closer, stroking his finger down Archie's spine, causing Archie to spin and face him.

"Are you in here crying, you little deaf pussy?" Henry said, moving his mouth slowly and exaggeratedly. Henry reached both hands for Archie's pants, trying to unclasp them. Archie swatted hard at him.

"What, you don't like that?" he said. Archie desperately tried to read his lips. "You used to like that a lot, remember? When we were just wittle chaps?"

Before Archie could comprehend the words, Henry slammed him into an open bathroom stall and frantically unbuttoned his own pants. Archie's lip popped on the toilet seat, his tears mixing with blood as he tried to form the words "please no," the blood spraying the seat red beneath his face. His hands still bloodied from before, he wiped the blood from his face, adding red to red.

"Stop" bubbled from Archie's bleeding lips, but Henry's strong hands positioned Archie's hips. Henry ripped Archie's undergarments from his body, shredding them. But then . . . it stopped. The way the night wind does at the coming of dawn.

The moment Archie dreaded never came, the ripping of his clothes, the forthcoming pain, the humiliation . . . there was nothing. It just ended.

As Archie turned to see Henry, he knew Henry

had seen his deepest secret. Finally, a lamp had been lit in the darkest parts of who he was.

"Oh my god, what is that?" Henry said to himself in disbelief.

There, between Archie's legs, a bulbous grouping of pus-filled boils and lumps had taken residence. The plague had seized Archie and settled upon his groin, thighs, and stomach. It looked as if eggs had been planted beneath his skin, oozing their goblin yolk, moist and damp.

When Henry realized what he had touched, he looked at his hands as if seeing them for the first time.

"You son of a bitch! You filthy son of a bitch!" Henry yelled. He brought his infected fists down upon Archie like a contaminated chimp. Archie tried hard to pull his pants up, receiving the pounds as if he deserved them, weeping—a mind ready for dying.

Then, as his vision turned red and his mind went black, he saw what no one wanted to see or could ever describe—a child being eaten.

He saw a slow-motion Armageddon before his very eyes. A nuclear explosion of fur and flesh mushroomed before him from nowhere and everywhere.

Henry was on his back on the checkered bathroom floor, his own pants down to his ankles, revealing his genitals. They too were a buffet for the beasts.

Archie couldn't hear Henry's screaming, but he could feel it—a vibration blooming from the apocalypse. It felt like relief, the lancing of a wound, the warm sun on a cold face. A smile formed on Archie's face as he watched the rats pump themselves into the bathroom from every vent and hole. Archie raised his arms in worship, allowing the friction to warm him. He lifted his foot to slam it upon Henry's jaw, but before he could join in the beating, one of the sisters exploded into the bathroom, grabbing Archie. She stomped the rats beneath her feet, one after another.

"Don't hurt them!" Archie stammered with his neglectful tongue and bloody lips.

Beneath the sister's boots, the rats popped like tomatoes.

"No! Don't hurt them!" Archie groaned louder and louder. He let out an animal-like scream. "Don't hurt them!"

The sister swatted at Archie's ankles and elbows

as the rats quickly made their way up his body. She dragged the boy into the hall. When they had made it out the door, three more staff rushed into the bathroom.

Archie looked from afar at his attacker drowning in a murky sea of brown and black fur. As the door swung back and forth, each sway showed a flicker of Henry's extinction from the flesh. The door swung, tissue; the door swung, the blinding white bone licked clean.

After it was over, Archie returned to his room, leaving the school staff to pull the fleshless child from the foamy mess of hair and blood, themselves getting bitten and scratched in the process. He reached into his pocket, and with his first finger, he stroked the top of Puck's head with a new sensation. A Shakespearean revelation of biblical proportions birthed itself from a blackened cocoon, which undulated within his bubonic-laced heart . . . *"Nature teaches beasts to know their friends."*

● ● ●

Before Dot could roll away from the table toward the screams, Francis sat down. His tray of food collided gently with the table, awakening Wenty to someone's presence. But Wenty already knew who it was. The invisible cosmic pull of Francis was all too familiar now. "Francis?"

"Yes, Wenty, it's Francis," Dot said with annoyance. But before Dot could shoo him away like an intruding hornet, he spoke for the first time.

"Tell me, children," Francis said with a quiet but harsh tone. Francis's voice jarred Dot and Wenty. He sounded as if his lungs had been charred and filled with ash—a voice unfit for a child, or stolen from a distant being. His purpled tongue was bright between his lipless mouth. His small teeth fenced it back as if it was too big for his hole. "What do you wish for?"

"Holy shit, the wanker speaks," Dot said, surprised by the fire boy's decision to finally communicate. "I knew it," she said more confidently.

To the children, this question felt both immature and wildly hopeful. Each of them wanted to talk and dream of things beyond but was just waiting for someone to ask. They wanted to be heard. To be thought of. But this question felt off. Wrong even. "What?" Dot shot back. She did not know if it was the questioner or the question that ignited her, forcing her to roll back to the table.

"Tell me, girl, what do you wish for?" he repeated, his smile returned, the one that had haunted Dot's dreams.

Dot knew exactly what her greatest wish was— and had always been. To run. To run hard and fast away from this dungeon. From these rats. This chair. It was a wish so intimate, so fragile, that to speak it would break it apart in her mouth.

"I know what I'd wish for," Wenty said, picking at his blind man's cane.

"Don't bother, Wenty. Wishes are for shooting stars and fairy tales," Dot snarled.

"And who's to say fairy tales aren't true?" said Francis.

"Jesus Christ, what are you talking about, you overbaked buttknuckler?" Wenty said, pushing himself away from the table. Just the sound of the fire boy's voice was enough to put Wenty on edge.

"You wish for a life more than Blackburn's, correct? A life beyond slop and rats?" Francis asked as memories of Claire seared through Dot's consciousness.

"Yes, and didn't you hear? Sister Carrie said an exterminator would be here in a couple of days. So that's a start."

"An exterminator isn't what you want, Dorothy," Francis said, poking at his filthy cast with his fork. His voice was slightly irritated.

"Actually, that's *exactly* what I want."

"You don't understand," Francis whispered back, still distracted by his cast. "No one ever understands . . . until it's too late." Dot didn't understand why, but Francis felt wiser than his age—as if he was hiding wisdom or harboring a secret like a moth in a glass jar.

"It seems like *you're* the one who doesn't understand," Wenty snorted, trying to find Archie's abandoned taters by palming the table in front of him.

"The problem isn't your rats. It's you," Francis said, his large black eyes fixating on the girl's.

Before she could answer, in the distance, Dot could see Archie marching away from the commotion, his face covered in so much blood it looked as if he was wearing a crimson mask. "Holy shit, Archie!" Dot exclaimed and immediately wheeled herself toward her friend, leaving the other abandoned with the fire boy.

"Dot! What happened? Wait! Don't leave me with—"

"You know, Wentworth, I've been meaning to speak with you," Francis interrupted as he pressed the fork deeper into his cast, the sound shaking Wenty's spine. "I've been watching you."

"ARCHIE! WHAT HAPPENED?" Dot cried out, wheeling quickly to his side. Archie could sense she was there but was left uncaring, as a shark would to a minnow. Dot grabbed his shirt and flung Archie around. She was met with a swift and sharp smack to her face. It was such a moment of shock, it felt as if even the rats in the walls went quiet from the echo of the betrayal. Archie stood there with his hand still in the motion of the follow-through, his bloody knuckles high toward heaven.

"dOOon yew eVa taWk toOo Mey agin"

Dot's eyes were large and wet, her hand to her cheek, soothing the sting. "Archie?" she whispered with newfound fear.

Archie brought the hand back across the other cheek and spit bloody saliva on Dot's legs. "eVer AgaiNnnn," he slurred as scarlet ooze dripped from his chin.

Dot could see a distant fire in his eyes, something blazing within the deaf boy. Darkness came to the surface of his skin, leaking through, and it frightened her. Not the way dead babies and unruly rats did. Its freight lay in its unknowing. Rats eat, people die, that's knowable. Archie's eyes were filled with flames of uncertainty, an ocean with no shore, a devil with no hell.

As Dot watched and waited for Archie to make his next move, the rats began again, like the start of rain. The scurry through the walls drowned out the noise of Dot's fears. It was a chilling reminder that the rats were spreading more than disease here.

"DO YOU KNOW WHAT I AM?" the fire boy asked.

"What?" Wenty listened, unsure of whether to try and run or stay put and make himself unseen like prey, the way a rabbit would hide beneath a bushel, sniffing the air.

"What I look like. Has anyone described to you my . . . *condition*?"

Wenty squirmed uncomfortably. "Dot said you were in a fire or something like that."

"Very good. Yes, I was in a fire."

Wenty nodded, trying to allow the conversation to fizzle.

"But it wasn't the fire that made me like this. It was my mother and father. They had other matters greater to them than their own children. They are no longer here."

"What happened?"

"They took from me, and I took from them."

Wenty chuckled. "What?"

"So, you wished for your parents to be gone, and it worked?"

"In a way."

"Bullshit."

Francis made a clicking sound, as if disappointed with Wenty's unspoken thoughts. "The problem is you don't see the problem. Well, you don't see much of anything, do you?" Francis joked, giggling to himself—a horrible sound to Wenty's ears. "You said you wish for eyes to see, yes?"

Wenty stayed silent, but his face gave away his response. Children and staff continued to run by screaming, and other nuns shut the doors to the dining hall, locking the children in. None of this fazed the blind boy. If anything, it allowed for greater silence, giving Francis his full attention.

"But, why do you wish to see?"

Wenty didn't know how to answer that. He would have thought it was obvious. As he was thinking of an answer, he realized he didn't know. Words failed to express his desire.

"I see what you can't," Francis said, licking his

lips. "I was like you, Wentworth. Then I met her. She came to me. Made me new. Whole. That's what you want, right? Wholeness?"

"From what I hear . . . you don't exactly look *whole*."

"To save one's life, one must lose it."

"Matthew 16:25," Wenty added to Francis's quotation.

"Very good, you know the scriptures. So you understand that life comes through suffering."

"I don't understand what you want," Wenty said with a twinge of annoyance.

"I want you to believe."

"To believe?"

"In what I offer, like stalks that grow from beans or golden eggs."

"You actually believe in fairy tales?"

"I dwell within one," Francis said with a happiness to his voice, tearing at the cast's cloth.

For the first time, Wenty wanted the fire boy to continue.

"For centuries," Francis said, slithering closer to his point, "mankind has believed that spirits danced with human souls . . . for a price." Francis continued slicing a deep line down his filthy cast. The tearing cut through Wenty's ears.

"For a price?" Wenty's hands gripped his cane nervously. "What does that mean?"

"Huitzilopochtli, the war god, demanded his blood. Moloch demanded his infants. Zeus demanded his vows. Each promised to rule and reign. But there is another incubus that offers itself to the wanting. There is one who exists between safety and danger, between life and death, desire and possession. The goddess of the time between the years."

"I don't understand," Wenty said.

"If one makes a wish to this being, a wish so craved that they would make a sacrifice for divine intervention," Francis said as he cracked open his cast like a rib cage. The fire boy finally uncaged his stump of a hand. "Then she would *dance* with you."

"Because I too can wish and pay the price for it? I don't have any money, duh."

Before Wenty could continue, the smell of rot filled his nose, making him gag. Francis's fingers had been chopped at their stump, leaving little to no movement and dark emerald bruising. The small tips were black, as if burnt; the palm was filled with veins and covered in scratches.

"If this is real, why not make a wish to change your body?"

"Because I wished for something more infinite," Francis said, airing out his tips.

"Oh yeah? What did you wish for?" Wenty asked, feeling strong.

"Purpose," Francis said, slamming his stump to the table, making the spoons and forks shake against their trays.

The response hit Wenty like a cold breeze. "She? Who is this being?" he asked, trembling as he played the fire boy's game.

"I've already said too much."

"Wait, if this is real, is it possible for—"

Francis interrupted with a glint of hope in his voice, "It goes by many names. The Whistler, Luna, The Harvester, Frau Perchta, Schanbelperchten, Zulu, but my amma is best known as . . . The Belly Slitter."

The name ran down Wenty's arms in a wave,

making him shudder. His lungs grew and deflated rapidly at the visual of what that meant to a blind boy. Just because Wenty couldn't see didn't mean his imagination wasn't zealous. Wenty reached for his stomach and rubbed his soft skin, trying not to imagine it opened like a flesh curtain.

"This is idiotic. There is no way—"

"Watch your tongue," Francis said with a bite. "She can not be proved, neither from the cosmos nor from the depths of human existence. She proves herself *through* herself. Her revelation is the proof of gods, given by existence itself. No one can reveal her but herself alone. This god is learned in revelation. Don't try to comprehend her, you unseeing, ignorant bug."

"I . . . I . . ."

"You can't imagine such a being. Be glad you've lost your eyes, Wentworth."

"How?" oozed from Wentworth's lips.

"Prometheus's debt. The food of the gods."

Just then, Dot rolled back to the table. Wenty couldn't tell her eyes were red and her cheeks were pink.

"Is everything okay with Archie?" Wenty asked between Francis's horrifying gobbledygook.

"No, not real—Oh my god, your hand, Francis!"

"What was all that screaming?" Wenty asked, needing more to soothe his anxiety.

Francis stood from the table, leaving his cast to lay upon his slop and food tray like the rib cage of a dead animal.

"Wait, Francis, what does Prometheus's debt mean? What are you talking about?"

"Once you learn of it, all will be revealed. I can't give you revelation; it must be unveiled by your own desire," he said as he looked one more time at the blind boy. Francis gingerly picked up each knife and fork, hiding them in his shirt and pants. But before Dot could press into whatever the hell that was, Francis walked away, staring up toward the stained glass.

"Gross. What was that all about?"

Wenty turned away from Dot. "I think he's trying to help us." But something in his gut did not believe his own words.

"THE CORONER WON'T BE COMING TODAY," one of the nuns whispered sheepishly to Father Gregory.

"Jesus Christ, are you kidding me? Why?" The priest said, grabbing the nun's arm and bringing her to a shadowy corner.

Dot watched as the priest rubbed his eyes in frustration. Then in a swift, bird-like motion, the nun and Father Gregory picked up the wrapped body. There was no hiding it from the students any longer. It was an apocalypse for the world to see. This was their new reality, that death could come at any moment. The smell of heaven and hell was closer than the scent of the potatoes in the dining hall. They had a newfound revelation that these walls could break in, and the oily-haired demons beyond them could take them.

Dot continued to watch from her chair, whispering in Wenty's ear, trying to keep the descriptions quiet in the silent, grieving hallway. The only noise came from the nun's boots and the satin sheet flapping around the corpse. They carried the body of their classmate, Henry, like pallbearers to the school's boiler room—the most private room in the entire school. It was too hot for rats and too dark for children. Dot and the boys had never ventured into the room out of fear and rumored ghost stories.

"They're carrying out what's left of Henry Broomfield in his bedsheet. Everyone around is watching, scared," Dot spoke gently in Wenty's ears. Her hot breath both soothed and bothered him. But something beyond fear and trembling was stirring in Wenty's chest, an energy he'd never felt before. It felt as if his insides had been replaced with hot coals. After speaking with Francis and hoping for a resolution, he did for himself what he'd always wanted to do for Dot—be brave.

"Where's Archie?" Wenty asked loudly.

"*Ssshhh*. I don't know," Dot whispered, fearing the worst.

"Dot, tell me, are you scared?" Wenty whispered back, realizing his volume.

Dot hated this question. She was always the

strong one and secretly enjoyed the reputation that came along with it, but in this moment, she let herself be known. "I've never been more scared of anything else in my entire life. For you, for me, and for Archie."

As Wenty heard the words leave her mouth, the coals in his chest were stoked once more. He stiffened his back, readjusted the waist of his pants, and leaned into Dot's ear one last time. "Meet me at Purgatory, immediately. We can fix this." Wenty said, exhaling his smoky, hot breath with a new air of confidence. Dot wasn't used to it, and she turned away from the action at the determined tone in his voice. The blind boy stood and marched through the crowd of onlookers as if he had new eyes.

ARCHIE SAT BENEATH THE BLANKETS on his bed, his bloody face full of fury and pain. Between his trembling palms sat Puck, his tail intertwining between Archie's fingers like yarn. Archie's mind pulsed with fear of what he'd just done—and what would be done.

He crumbled stale crackers and peppered them on his sheets, allowing Puck to nibble and lick the crumbs. Archie watched the rat, its unassuming nestling and twitches reminding him that these aren't dangerous creatures like everyone thinks. They are just misunderstood. They were creatures that loved him and protected him—like with Henry. They're not hurting others; they are saving them. They're not to be feared but befriended.

Archie could feel his heart pounding harder and harder, like a cathedral bell ringing from his center.

Then, in a moment of intoxication, Archie did something he'd never done before. He had the urge to bring Puck closer to himself, close to his bloody lips, allowing their eyes to connect. He could feel the current of electricity between himself and the beast, like planets and moons aligning.

Archie stuck his tongue out and began licking, grooming, Puck. From the top of his head to his hind legs. He sucked on his tail like a noodle and rubbed Puck's chin gingerly. Archie could feel in his gut that they were closer now—becoming one. Puck was now closer to the deaf boy than his own breath, making Archie smile between licks as saliva and rat hair drained out the sides of his mouth. He never wanted this moment to end, but then something occurred that had only happened in Archie's fairy tale literature readings and dreams. As he was being caressed by Archie's bubblegum pink tongue, Puck turned around, placed his paws on Archie's cheeks . . . and spoke.

"Archibald . . . Moonchild, it's time."

PUCK

*There was nothing particularly wrong
with them;
They were just the ordinary garden variety of
human garbage.*

—Robert Penn Warren

DOT'S PIPE HAD ALREADY BEEN LIT for a minute before Wenty found his way to their spot after grabbing his jacket from his bedside. They both stood there in the quiet, allowing their tobacco smoke to fill the silence.

"Did you get Archie?" Wenty asked.

"No, I couldn't find him," Dot said, lying as she exhaled. She would never tell Wenty of Archie's violence, fearful of what it could do to him, what it could do to their friendship.

"Okay. Either way, I have a plan," Wenty said, tamping his tobacco. "Or at least I hope it's a plan."

"Okay, for what?"

"Francis told me—"

"Francis?" Dot shouted through the smoke. "Is this a joke? You're friends with crispy-face now?"

"No, he terrifies me. But he told me about something or someone who can help us."

"An exterminator is coming. What else would we need to do?"

"This isn't about the rats anymore, Dorothy!" Wenty shouted.

Dot had never heard Wenty use her full name. This too was a revelation of how Wenty was changing. She hated it and admired it at the same time.

"Francis told me all we have to do is make a certain kind of wish—a wish with an offering—and something will come and grant us our deepest wants."

Smoke left Dot's nose like a curious animal as her eyes fixated on Wenty's face. Wenty waited in silence for her response. To his chagrin, she exploded with laughter. In that moment, he thanked God he was blind because if he saw the girl he loved laughing at his expense, it'd end him.

"Yeah? And you, out of all people, believe that piss-flap? Jesus, Wenty, I thought you were more reasonable than that."

Wenty could feel the white knight within himself shrivel. He also struggled to believe Francis's words, but the need to believe in something greater than himself was stronger.

"Fuck you, Dorothy," Wenty said, exhaling and dumping the tobacco out of his pipe.

A prick of darkness poked Dot's mind like a scorpion sting. The thought of losing two friends in one day was too much. They were her only family. She could see she'd gone too far, and to save the moment, to save the friendship, she played into the drama.

"I'm sorry, I shouldn't have laughed. But if it wasn't a wish to exterminate these fucking rats, then what?"

With a burst, Wenty's words exploded. "For you to run, god dammit! For me to see you run! For us and Archie to be able to live! Remember my vision of the orange moon above the red grass?" Dot never had the heart to tell him grass was green. "Remember how I could see us holding hands, how for the first time I felt warm, like there was actually something living inside of me?" Wenty's voice broke, and emotion choked him. "I don't know why, but for some reason I feel that this is our chance to bring that to reality, Dorothy."

"Where would we even go? It's not like we can get money or get on a boat or—"

"Who cares? At least we'll all be together, finally made right."

"I don't understand how any of this—"

"I don't either," Wenty interrupted, "but for the first time, I feel hope."

The gravity of the situation seized them both, sucking the cold air out of their lungs. This was no longer a fantasy but a real-life chance in front of them. An invitation from God.

"Wenty . . . Okay, fine, let's make a wish. What exactly do we have to offer if not money?" Dot asked, assuming there was no harm in playing with childish magic.

"Well, that's the problem. Francis said 'the sin of Prometheus,' that's how we'll know what to offer."

"Like the myth?" Dot said, relighting her pipe with a struck match.

"A myth?" Wenty asked with excitement. Dot always knew more than he did.

"Yeah. The Roman or Greek story?"

"I don't know it."

"Neither do I. I just know that name."

"How can we find out?" Wenty asked, squeezing his cane.

"Fuck's sake, I don't know, a stupid book?"

Wenty kicked himself. "Of course, the library! Let's go!"

"Wait! Jesus, Wenty," Dot said, grabbing the blind boy's arm. "Why do you think he's trying to help us? What does he have to gain? Don't you find all of this a bit odd?"

"I don't know. Maybe he wants friends? Maybe he's not as bad as he seems?"

"Or maybe," Dot interrupted, "he'll want a payment of his own."

The thought arrested Wenty's momentum. Dot could see his eyes beneath his bandage rolling back and forth with possibilities. As she took one last drag, she saw it again, next to Wenty's feet. The dandelion. Up from the aging snow and frozen ground had sprung another white, puffed flower. It floated there like a planet, barely noticeable against its winter canvas. As Dot stared at it curiously, she realized it wasn't just one. Bundles of them erected out of the ice around them, like a cumulus flying above the arctic, leading like footsteps to hills just beyond the school.

"Do you see that?"

"Ha ha, very funny," Wenty barked sarcastically.

"Sorry . . . but there are dandelions everywhere," Dot said, reaching down to pick one up.

"So?"

"So? It's winter. Don't you find that insane?" she said, examining the weed's feather-like foliage. Her mind drifted to Francis. "Don't you remember? Francis had one of these in his pocket on Ramp Day."

"Big deal. He must have picked it up on his way in."

"Beyond fucking weird that these are blooming in winter, right?"

"God, who cares? We have bigger things to worry about!"

"I remember my grandfather said that if you can blow all their seeds off in one puff, that'll grant you a wish."

Wenty looked in Dot's direction with a hint of annoyance, feeling she was downplaying his new-found hope.

Dot placed the dandelion in Wenty's hand. "Maybe we should just do this instead of finding Francis?"

Wenty gave her a small smile out of the corner of his mouth and gingerly placed the weed in his front coat pocket.

"Come on, we're going to be late for choir," Dot said, rolling over the dandelions.

"What about the library?" Wenty said earnestly.

"Tonight, after dark. But we can't now. I can't go back to Father Gregory's again. Never again."

Wenty knew she would win with that argument every time. "Okay, fine. I'll be there shortly. Go on ahead without me," Wenty yelled after her as she made her way to the school's arched doors.

He waited until the door was completely shut before jiggling the handle of the garden shed door— it was unlocked. The blind boy carefully stepped in, grazing his fingers over the many objects in the cold room. Textures of soil and terracotta kissed his fingers until he finally felt what he was after: cold steel. It was sharp and smooth. Wentworth gave a small nod of accomplishment, sliding the awl into his trouser pocket. He was starting to enjoy the feeling of courage as blood rushed through his veins.

• • •

Through the stained glass window in his office, Father Gregory watched as two children snuck away to their "secret" hiding space behind the gardener's shed. There, he could see by the intensity of their expressions that their discussions were heavy. They seemed like they carried the weight of the world.

"Do you see those children out there smoking behind the shed?" Father Gregory asked Sister Margaret. "Is that Dorothy and Wentworth?"

The nun perched higher to see around the shed. Both were a bit fatigued from carrying the body of a dead child.

"Oh yes," she said between heavy breaths. "Those children are like locusts, Father. Wherever they go, surely pestilence follows."

"You really believe that, Sister?"

"With all my heart. That's why all of the—"

"Our children are dropping like stars. We still have no documentation for the most recent newcomer, and we have three more days until the extermination. Smoking children are the least of our worries. At least they're alive."

"I'm sorry. You're right, Father."

"I'm worried for you, Sister. I've seen your heart growing hard these past few months," the Father said in a moment of warmth. "Where is that tenderness you fruited upon your arrival?"

"Well, I guess I just, umm . . ." the nun searched within herself, fearful of what she might find. "I guess these are trying times for my school and children."

"*His* school."

"Of course, you're right. This is the Lord's home."

"Be on guard, Sister. I worry for you. I pray for you."

"Thank you, Father. Although . . ."

"Yes?"

"Dorothy does know of *the infant*," the nun whispered, "but I'm guessing that doesn't really matter now, given what happened to Henry Broomfield?"

Father Gregory looked at Sister Margaret with eyes colder than winter. "Tell me, is she telling the other students?"

"She threatened that she might," the nun said sheepishly.

"Dorothy, Dorothy, Dorothy, after all we've been through . . ."

Sister Margaret looked painfully at the father, unaware of what to say.

He gave a nod. "Bring her to my study after dinner. Thank you, Sister," he said, picking his teeth with his pinky and sucking off his nails the remnants from lunch. Something he did when he was anxious about something, the sister had noticed. He gave the nun a final look of determination.

Sister Margaret's eyes squirmed regrettably back toward the unknowing children.

"MOONCHILD, IT'S TIME."

Tears of disbelief rained down Archie's eyes, his pupils eclipsing their redness.

"Can you hear me?" Puck asked.

"pAwUcccK?" Archie said through slobber and snot, forming a large smile on his round, bloodied face.

"There you are. You can hear me," Puck said. The hair and whiskers around his cone-like mouth curved to face the heavens.

Archie was so stunned at first by his pet speaking to him that he neglected to realize he was also *hearing* him. "Wey kun I heEr yew?"

"Because we have finally become one flesh, a cosmic collision, my moonchild," Puck whispered, raising himself onto two feet and lifting his front paws up high from beneath the sheet. "Archibald, when two stars orbit each other closely, they share the same atmosphere. Then the two flaming suns merge, resulting in a luminous red nova. You and I are that nova." Puck continued to rub his tiny rodent paws against Archie's cheeks, the way a mother would to a newborn.

"But hOw Is this reAl?" Archie asked, wiping his eyes.

"Because it is time."

"TymE? For wut?"

Archie watched Puck's eyes roll in their sockets, spinning like orbiting comets. From their core, a distant light kindled and grew as the rat's eyes pulsated in rhythm. Archie could feel himself urinate and drool, every orifice opening itself to the manifestation. A catatonic sleep overtook him, but he remained sensitive to the universe held within Puck's gaze. Archie wanted to worship and sing, but as he raised his hands to touch Puck's, he only felt himself.

His disease was growing—his fingertips grazed over newfound bulbs budding on his neck and chin.

The Black Plague had fully come to Blackburn's.

MAYOR

"MR. MAYOR?"

"Yes, Rosemary, come in."

"I found someone to help with our . . . *problem.*"

"Wonderful! Who is he? What is he?"

"He's an Empiric."

"Excuse me?"

"A plague doctor," Rosemary said, swallowing the uncomfortableness in her throat.

"I've never heard of such a—"

"It's a growing profession in light of the recent outbreaks. Apparently, he has a poison of some kind that can extinguish the vermin."

"Well, now you have my attention," the mayor said, standing from his desk. "Come in and shut the door. Now tell me, how much does he want?"

"Well, that's the thing. The doctor said all bargaining will commence at the end of his duty," she said gently, shutting the door behind her.

"So he could be quite expensive?"

"Or he could be quite affordable."

"When can he start?"

"Now."

The mayor walked to his drink cart and filled a cup with brown liquor, which he quickly consumed. Rosemary watched the glass hit his teeth, clinking them like a toast. Then with a small hiccup, he said, "Send him out there, let him do his thing, and we'll pay whatever the hell we want to pay. Damn fool doesn't know how to bargain."

"Mr. Mayor, with all due respect, I don't think that's wise. I'd rather not hire him if this is your plan."

"Do you want a drink, Rosemary?" the mayor asked with a foreign tone.

"No, I'm fine, but as I was saying—"

"Here, take it. You have to have one with me to celebrate! You found our exterminator and saved the election!"

"I'm not sure there is much to celebrate," Rosemary said, taking the glass in her hand. But the mayor didn't loosen his grasp around the tumbler. Instead he hugged her fingers with his large chimp-like hands, allowing the drink and glass between their hands to grow warm.

"God, I hate when you open your mouth," the mayor whispered as he applied pressure to Rosemary's grip on the drink. The intensity between them caused her hand to shake. Small cracks formed, and Rosemary could feel the cup between her fingers break into pieces. A thousand tiny swords entered her skin.

"Why don't pretty girls keep the top hole closed and open the bottom one, hmm?" the mayor whispered.

Rosemary shrieked in pain as the mayor put his free hand over her mouth, slamming her against the closed office door, shushing her as she whimpered from the glass penetrating her soft flesh. The spirit, mixed with blood, fell to the floor. When Rosemary stopped her instinctual scream, the mayor released his grip.

"Fuck you," Rosemary said, attending to her hand, its pink skin resembling star-shaped flesh, stinging and dripping from its center.

"Make it happen, or I'll see where else I can

place sharp glass within your tight little body," the mayor said, pouring himself another drink. "And dispose of this fucking dead baby, will you?" the mayor said, pointing to the trash bin near his desk.

Those who wish to sing always find a song.

—Swedish Proverb

Come, Holy Ghost, Creator blest,
And in our hearts take up Thy rest;
Come with Thy grace and heav'nly aid
To fill our hearts which Thou hast made,
To fill our hearts which Thou hast made.

O Comforter, to Thee we cry,
Thou heav'nly gift of God most high;
Thou fount of life, and fire of love,
And sweet anointing from above,
And sweet anointing from above.

Praise be to Thee, Father and Son,
And Holy Spirit, Three in one;
And may the Son on us bestow
The gifts that from the Spirit flow,
The gifts that from the Spirit flow.

BLACKBURN'S CHILDREN SANG LOUDLY but woefully. No tenors or altos, just noise spilling from their mouth holes as the choir instructor waved her hands in a half-hearted attempt to compose the disaster. The nun often reminded herself that God loves to listen to all his children sing, no matter their ability.

As the nun guided the children through the hymn, her eyes landed on Dot, who had decided not to join the chorus today. "Stop, children," she said, forming her hand into a tight fist. "Dorothy, if you seek to pass this class, you must sing."

The children turned to face the quiet girl, adding a new layer of uncomfortableness.

"I know your legs don't work, but do your lips?" the nun asked sarcastically.

"Respectfully, Sister, I don't sing. And I don't care about passing this class," Dot said. The past few days had broken her, the way one might break a wild mustang.

"Dot, just be chill," Wenty whispered out of the corner of his mouth. He felt that part of protecting Dot was helping her find the right moments to battle—this *not* being one of them.

"No, that's okay, Wentworth. I can handle a smidge of pushback. In fact I welcome it. Dorothy, why don't you care about singing? It's good for the soul. It releases all that's within you into the world and actualizes it. It makes your emotions real. God put music into the world so that when words fail, songs are born." The kids around Dot giggled as the teacher glittered her fingers to enhance her point.

"My emotions *are* real, and right now, they're sad they have to participate in singing to a god or ghost who doesn't give any attention to us. So I will not sing, Sister. Plus, this song is weird as hell." This sparked a commotion of laughter among the children.

The nun, knowing the pigheadedness that was Dorothy, smiled. Then, making her way through the children, she stood over Dot and brought her mouth to her ear. "Fine. Why don't you roll yourself down to Father Gregory's room and tell him you'll be joining him rather than today's chorus." Dot's eyes grew in fear.

"Oh, you don't like that idea? Should have thought about that before you decided you're too good for my class. Bye-bye," the nun said, forcefully rolling Dot around to face the exit.

"I'll go too!" Wenty shouted at the nun.

"No, no, Mr. Wentworth. Dorothy doesn't want to sing with others, so she doesn't get punished with others."

Unable to think of a way out, Dot left the music room like a passing ghost, wheeling by Francis on the far left of the choir stand. She gave him a small nod as the fire boy gave a haunting smirk, as if he knew something she didn't.

● ● ●

As Dot knocked on the priest's door, her insides hurt. Each bang against the door felt like a rifle shot to her ears.

"Enter," Father Gregory said.

"Hello, Father."

"Well, hello, Dorothy," the priest said with a saddened smile.

"Sister Anne told me I had to come down here and be with you since I chose not to participate in singing."

"Did she now? I've been meaning to be with you anyway. I wasn't expecting you until after dinner, but now is just as good."

Dot could feel the air leaving her lungs. His words were a serpent tightening around her. Her eyes searched for anything in the room other than his, caterpillaring between each of the bricks that made up his large study.

"Sister Margaret informed me that you threatened her. Is that true?" the priest said, moving to the front of his desk and leaning on it comfortably.

This was the only room where Dot felt her sarcasm and stubbornness could come back to bite her, which pushed her toward truth. "I told her I knew of *the infant*, if that's what you mean."

"It's not, and you know it," the priest replied, taking a silver jewelry box from the shelf and laying it on his lap. Dot could see the sparkling emeralds and sapphires arrayed in the pattern of a white dove. A mosaic bird clasped a branch between its carnelian beak, a biblical sign of life beyond the storm—a light beyond the shadowed path.

"You threatened that you'd tell the children about our little infant issue, and when others know, officials get worried. And when officials get worried, they close things down. And when things get closed down, students get shipped off and teachers become unneeded . . . You can see the progression," the priest said with broken words. "Everything you and I have been working for would come to an end."

"I wouldn't tell anyone, I promise!" Dot said frantically. "I can make it up to you, the way you like."

The priest ignored the lame girl's plea and opened the jeweled box. Slowly, he pulled out Dot's rosary beads and held them up. All fifty-nine spheres glistened in the afternoon sun.

"Shall we?" the priest offered.

"I can't keep doing this. I hate this," Dot said, rolling her chair away from the sacrament.

"I know, my dear girl, I know," the priest said, bringing a chair close to her to be nearer to her. "But

I care about you . . . and prayer, worship, and hope can bring praise from pain. That is my purpose with our time."

"You've been trying to get me to pray, to walk, to sing, to—" Dot shook at the thought. "I'm begging you, can we *please* stop this?"

The priest pulled back, eyes slanting toward the earth. "Dorothy," the priest said, sensing newfound desperation. "Of course we can stop praying together, but I will not stop praying for you. That's all I have to give. It's the best of what I have to give . . ." He allowed his words to trail off as he placed her beads back into the special box he had made for her years earlier. "Have you told your friends what we do here? Our times of prayer and confession and sacrament?"

"No," Dot said, shrinking into herself, picking at her chair's handrest.

"Are you still ashamed?" Dot nodded without looking up. "Oh, daughter. Why?"

"Wouldn't you be?" Dot said, turning her wheelchair toward the flickering votives. "I'm so sick of thinking something will change these," she said, bringing her fist down upon her unfeeling legs. It shook the candles before her, extinguishing one, re-

leasing its soul into the air. For Dot, this was a metaphor for her final prayer, like smoke.

"Hope is a doctrine for fools," the priest whispered, striking a match and resurrecting the candle.
"Beckoning one to live beyond what they can see,
know, or accomplish." He handed Dot a handkerchief. "But to live without hope is to cease to live.
Hell is hopelessness."

Dot's flesh crawled, wanting to tear itself apart as
she tried to pull away, but the power was too strong
for her, and her tears broke the steel dam of her
pride. Dorothy wailed as the priest prayed over her.
He embraced her tenderly, fatherly. "It's okay. You
are so loved, my child."

The two held each other as a mass was lit amid
the underworld that was Blackburn's. "Father, why
is it so hard for me to pray? To sing? To believe?"
the girl asked with volcanic eyes.

The priest was at a loss for words at Dot's vulnerability. He relied on God's word and whispered to
the child he cared for so deeply, "All that rings true,
all that commands reverence, and all that makes for
right; all that is pure, all that is lovely, all that is gra-

cious in the telling; virtue and merit, wherever virtue and merit are found—let this be your thoughts."

This shook the girl alive again in pain and hope—and she hated every moment of it.

Not knowing when the dawn will come,
I open every door.

—Emily Dickinson

"WE WATCH YOU DREAM. We have since everlast-
ingness was laid in our cosmos's vast frame. Time
is above and absorbed, of which none can force or
shake. Do you feel it in your eyes yet, Archibald?
The frantic muse of heaven's stately lights penetrating them? New moons of old suns. Constellations
welcome you. They are your light-bringers. The Sun
has left its heart for you. A golden kernel. Receive it
in you. Open to it. The sable mantle sets upon your
brow, bright crevices with no shadows. Red shadows
bleed. In Gothic splendor, the angels and demons
relieved at your birth with their queer twinkling
tears; shed your eyes, Archibald. Give them your
eyes, Archibald. Give those Promethean orbs, noble
fire, nightly gazes, frigid spheres, your long hidden
shapes and death to our Maker's praise. The oceans
lean on the sky in wait. Can you feel it yet? Can you

smell your new eyes yet? They are like transpicuous air, terrestrial moons, red swans. Be the stars. See them in you. I see them. I see them. I see them. They enlighten new fields and our new inhabitants. This is the land of the living. Do you see it yet? All these illustrious worlds wait for your command. Thousands, like glass, lost in the wilds of vast chill, seek the superior sway. Give over your eyes so our new planets of various magnitudes can finally obey."

Puck removed his wet mouth from deep in Archie's ears, licking its whiskers as he bent them inward to his cone-shaped hole. The rat was out of breath from its prayer. Archie lay in the bluing snow as fresh dandelions erected around him. One by one, they came beneath the night sky, their color reminiscent of nuclear smoke.

Archie lay prostrate on his back, arms splayed out like the crucifix that dangled above the school's blackboards. His mauveine and cosmic eyes spun like soaring orbs, and distant stars came to nova and sprayed within them. Within each fleshy sphere, an entire evolution was taking place, creature to man to devil in perfect conception.

Puck licked himself and watched the transfiguration, rubbing his fur head here and there against the boy's soft blue cheeks. Puck pushed himself back from the boy as the ground swayed like waves and Archibald was raised from the snow beneath—stretched in the frosted air, suspended, flying, soaring. This shook the boy alive again in pain and hope . . . and he embraced every moment of it.

"There you are, my moonchild," Puck whispered in eternal glory.

WENTY'S GROIN BEGAN TO GROAN. He had no idea what time it was, but judging by the silence and gentle breaths from the neighboring beds, he assumed dawn had not broken. He pushed his fingers to the glass window beside his bed, trying to feel the sun's eastern warmth, but the glass felt like ice. His bladder burned like acid.

Dammit, he thought.

He reached under and patted for his bedpan. Something he rarely used out of fear that Dot might see. Suddenly, the thought of reaching into the abyss beneath his bed made his head hurt with nerves. So Wenty broke curfew by quickly bolting for the washroom, abandoning his walking cane, and staying close to the gravelly walls instead.

The school was quiet except for the ever-present rumbling in the corridor walls, which only intensified his fear. After finally arriving and pulling his pants down, he could think with greater clarity just how stupid it was for him to go the bathroom during such a dangerous time. But there was a splinter of pride in that condemnation. Wenty doing daring things was still rare.

As he sat there on the cold porcelain seat pissing, he wondered if he was fearful of most things due to blindness or if he was just plain terror-stricken. *I'm not a boy at all but a worm. I must become a man.*

A distant sound broke his self-deprecation. It wasn't the sound of vermin or machine, but someone awake. Wenty tried hard to stop his flow, stinging his crotch. He could finally hear what it was—the sound of shuffling feet. Someone was scurrying toward him.

He quickly finished and lifted his feet off the ground. He sat cross-legged on the toilet, fearful it was the rats again. The sound came again from the far end of the school's hallway—footsteps. Someone was running in his direction. The footfalls beat louder as if whoever it was wasn't trying to hide his intentions, the sound in beat with Wenty's quickening heart. And then, the running stopped right outside the washroom door. Wenty heard the moaning of hinges opening slowly.

He cupped his mouth to hide his rapid breaths, listening to the footsteps across the tile floor. The intruder stopped outside the stall and waited.

"Hello?" Wenty asked softly.

"Have you seen the revelation yet of what you must sacrifice?" Francis whispered with angst.

"Fuck on a duck, Francis. Give me two minutes to piss." No noise from the fire boy. "Dot and I will figure it out tonight. We're going to the library, and then we'll come find you."

"Will your fat friend be joining you?" Francis asked. He whispered incomprehensible gibberish to himself outside the stall as if talking to someone who wasn't there.

"Giggy? God, no."

"No, the one who can't hear."

"Archie? I haven't been able to find him any-where," Wenty said. He realized just how long it had been since he'd seen his dear friend. "But yes, Archie will be joining us."

Wenty could hear the pitter-patter of Francis applauding outside the stall door.

• • •

Wenty searched for Dorothy the best way a blind boy could. Touching shadows, gripping the velvet dark, walking swiftly. Sweat beads formed on his forehead, his mind racing. Wenty opened the door and immediately whisper-shouted, "Dot! Dot, you here?"

"*Ssshhh*," a tired Giggy croaked from the corner.

"Giggy, I know that's you, you worthless dog fart. Stay out of this!" Wenty knew that'd shut him up.

"I'm so sick of you guys making fun of me. You're blind, and I don't make fun of you!" Giggy shot back through his own whisper-shout, a first for the boy.

"You really want to do this now, Gollumpus?" Wenty with another blow.

"No, I guess not."

"Then piss off," Wenty said. Patting Dot's bed, he felt her legs. They were smaller than he remembered, like twigs beneath leaves.

"Dot, thank goodness," Wenty said, out of breath. "It's time. We have to get to the library."

Wenty left Dot and reached beneath his box spring for his hidden awl. Dot still wasn't responding, but he could hear her shuffling.

"Dorothy, are you with me? Are you awake? Where's Archie? We need to wake Archie!"

Then she spoke, her voice distant and muddled, "I'm not up for this."

"What? Why?"

"I'm just, just . . ."

"What happened with that bastard?"

"Father Gregory? Nothing. I don't want to talk about it."

Wenty felt the animal inside him coming to the surface. "Listen, this is why we have to get to the library and figure this shit out. So we can escape."

Dot looked into his eyes as if they were there. As if she was the only one who could see them. She hugged her blind friend. "Why is everything coming apart?"

Wenty hugged her back, slowing himself. "Let's make sure *we* never do." And with that, the girl who couldn't walk and the boy who couldn't see moved through the shadows, making haste for the library.

IN HIS STUDY BY CANDLELIGHT, the priest took ink to paper and wrote his plea. Never in his forty years of ministry had he ever written a letter like this, but these were dire times, and his heart was breaking.

Dear Florence, words can't begin to express my hurt for you and what you saw. We didn't protect or help you, and for that I take the fullest responsibility. That child, the other children, the safety of the school, and of course, you.

This letter is written with the utmost urgency to implore your swift return to Blackburn's as soon as possible. Not for me or the staff, but for Dorothy the lame. The child we both adore at current is more like a husk—half a lady at this point. I've been told by the sisters that she asks day and night about your whereabouts, with which we have nothing to offer her comfort. Therefore, God willing, you shall return to us and your duties. We render to you the gratitude you deserve for your care of the children these many years and for the fidelity you have shown us. And with the full intention of worthily rewarding your services, we ask you to continue the same.

One final plea. Please return, if not for Dorothy, then for her soul. May the great and good God long preserve your majesty in safety.

Your majesty's most bounden and devoted,
Father Gregory Of Blackburn

*Inside my empty bottle I was constructing a
lighthouse while all others were making ships.*

—Charles Simic

DOT LIT A CANDLE AND HANDED it to the boy who could only see darkness. This was not for him; this was for her. He was to act as her lighthouse as they navigated the murky waters that led them toward their treasure.

"Quickly," Wenty whispered, knowing they were in more danger now than they had ever been.

"I still don't understand what we're looking for," Dot said, wheeling herself with greater speed.

"Neither do I, but what else can we do?" The candlelight formed large, foreboding shadows against Blackburn's crumbling walls, reminding Dot that they were not safe in this school at all. No one was. The shadows followed them like the nuns, watching over them, looming over them.

As Dot turned the large brass knob of the library's entrance, she realized it was locked. "Fuck," she whispered.

"Here," Wenty said, taking the awl from his pocket.

"Oh, wow. How did you know it would be locked?"

"Archie usually has to get a key from a teacher when he receives his books, so I just thought I'd make sure. We don't have time to waste."

Dot stared at the boy in the dark. His face was only half-lit by the candle, but she saw all of him. She felt something in her stomach, something beyond nerves, something beyond wonder . . . Attraction? She felt a primal pull toward Wenty for the first time. She could feel herself starting to sweat as her warm fingers touched his cold hands to receive the tool. This surprised her, and if she'd had the time, she may have explored this new feeling longer, but the task at hand was too sensitive. Too important. She pushed through the thoughts, returning to her duty. But not before Wenty noticed her hesitation.

"What's wrong?" Wenty asked.

"What? What do you mean?"

"Your breathing changed."

"No it didn't, and Jesus . . . that's creepy," Dot

deflected, penetrating the awl into the lock. "Don't listen to my breathing, you wanker." Wenty giggled, and even Dot smiled—an alien feeling to them both in light of current events. "There, got it!"

Blackburn's library was extensive for the school's size. It had been the parishioners' study in its previous life. Large candle chandeliers hung above their heads like shipwrecked ghosts, and the large wooden shelves evoked feelings of Roman pillars. Massive, ornate tapestries hung from wall to wall with images of Christ's sacrifice sewn in with what were once vibrant reds, blues, and yellow threads but were now bleached by decay and sunlight. Dot could still make out each of Jesus's wounds as they sparkled with golden fibers in the candlelight. She started to feel a sense of confidence as she strolled between the large cases. The room was quiet as death; even the spider's spindling in the corner was deafening to Wenty. "Where do we start?"

"I'm assuming Greek mythology and literature."

"What can I do to help?" Wenty asked, feeling useless at this moment.

"Just hold my light."

Wenty nodded and continued to hold onto Dot's chair as she slowly steered, mumbling to herself the titles of books as she passed her fingers along their spines. *"The Family, Farmer Giles of Ham, The First Princess of Wales, Flambards Confessions, The Gentle Falcon* . . . Here we are! *Greek Myth and Lore."*

"Oh shit, awesome," Wenty said eagerly. Wenty listened as Dot plopped the book on a nearby desk and flipped through its ancient pages.

"Here, I think I found something . . . *Then Olympian Zeus gathered up all fire and hid its flame from man."*

"Shit," Wenty whispered.

"What? You already figured it out?"

"Not exactly, but . . . fire."

"Yeah, so what?" Dot asked, wondering what she was missing.

"Francis was in a fire."

Dot had no response to Wenty's haphazard realization. All she could do was continue this godforsaken game the fire boy was playing. *"Prometheus knew that man could not survive without fire. In spite of the devastating power of Zeus' thunderbolt, clever Pro-*

metheus tempted the great Olympian's rage by daring to steal fire from the gods a second time."

"Okay, so the sin of Prometheus was he stole fire. I still don't get it. What was his punishment? Or debt?"

Dot flipped through the pages to the end of the chapter, where she came upon a rather horrific image. "Holy pisswizzard."

"What?"

"*. . . You will face an even more horrible torture, for Olympian Zeus will set his predatory eagle upon you. Each day, this greedy vulture will tear open your body and gorge his voracious appetite upon your defenseless liver. Each night, your liver will regenerate itself to provide a renewed feast for the eagle on the following day."*

"I don't understand," Wenty exhaled, accidentally extinguishing the fire he was holding. As darkness fell over the library, an intruder's voice broke the night. "Liver."

Dot jumped, dropping the book to the ground, the thundering noise reverberating through the corridor.

"Francis, what the hell?" Wenty yelled at the fire boy, trying to regain his composure.

"The Belly Slitter will only accept a liver as an offering," Francis said from the darkness, his most beloved place to be. Wenty and Dot watched as Francis's disfigured stump of a hand waved itself like a serpent in the air, coming close to his ear and then facing them as if it could see them, as if it moved independently from the arm it was attached to.

"So all of this was pointless? Because we're fresh out of liver, big guy, and I sure ain't giving up mine," Dot said to the darkness.

The clicking sound of disappointment hung in the air like a dying clock. "*Tsk, tsk, tsk* . . . I had higher hopes for you, Dorothy."

"Well, that was stupid. I'm a hurricane of disappointment," Dot ricocheted back.

"I never said it has to be *your* liver," Francis said. Dot strained to see Francis through the darkened room. She could just make out his leathery face in the sliver of moonlight as it twisted and contorted into a demented smile.

HUNDREDS OF RATS TWISTED AROUND his arms and legs, licking and caressing every bulbous wound and extended pore. His leakage was their milk. The hairy tentacles writhed and squeezed his body. Archie didn't know where he ended and the rats began. He was becoming a bridge between boy and beast.

He looked down in the darkened room, trying to decipher his own pink flesh. He brought his hand close to his face, but even his fingers were one with the swarming rats. Pale tails, black eyes, speckles of shit, matted brown fur—all a robe of transformation. Vermin hid beneath his clusters of pus-filled blisters and plagued joints as if they were rodent nests. Archie moaned at the feeling of it. He felt tickles and scratches from toes to eyes as Puck continued his sermons within Archie's dysfunctional ears. "You are the becoming now, seize the collapsing star," Puck coached through licks and hisses.

"WuT aM I beCUnING?" Archie whispered through a moan.

"*Hers*," Puck breathed into him. But before Archie could burst with wonderment, the rats that snaked around the boy startled and scurried into the library's shadows and corners. Puck and Archie strained to listen to the intruder entering as she wheeled herself across the aphotic room.

"Shhh, Moonchild, quickly hide. Someone is approaching."

Though she be but little, she is fierce.

—William Shakespeare

"YOU'LL HAVE TO CARRY ME," Dot said, raising her arms to Wentworth.

"I can't. I mean . . . I don't think I'll be able to," Wenty said with a speck of shame. "I'll need to hold onto the walls."

Dot looked past the blind boy as Francis stood there with a smile, applauding. Then the fire boy hefted the lame girl over his shoulder, abandoning the wheelchair at the top of the stairs.

The boiler room had infinite stone steps downward, leading to a place nestled against the gates of hell. Neither Wenty nor Dot had been down there, but Francis led the way in the darkness as if it was a familiar route.

Dot was dying within her own skin as Francis touched and gripped her, smelling his clothes that reeked of piss, smoke, and sweat. Both Dot and

Wenty's minds squirmed with curiosity as to why they were headed down here. Wenty assumed it was because it was out of sight from teachers and priests, or at least he hoped that was the reason.

Finally, Dot could see the red glow of the furnace and feel its radiant heat. It was louder than they expected and surprisingly small compared to what they imagined. There in hell lay a couple of small tables, an enormous blazing furnace, and stone-fixed walls. *It's no wonder the rats avoid it*, Dot thought. The heat was almost unbearable.

Francis placed Dot on one of the tables and grabbed Wenty's arm, guiding him to the girl. Once Dot situated herself, she could see this was more than just a boiler room. It was a bunker. There were scraps of food, a bucket full of human shit, and a small bit of bedding in the corner. "Fuck me, Francis. Is this where you've been hiding all this time?" It took her a moment to realize that Francis was waiting for something. His midnight eyes, wet and eager, locked onto Dot's. Dot was about to serve a cold dish of sarcasm before she finally saw what the fire boy was waiting for.

The boiler room had been redecorated.

Hand-painted images covered its stone walls. The red-painted lines were thin but glowed brightly from the light of the furnace. Dot could barely take it in. The cave-like drawings stretched from top to bottom, left to right, covering every inch of the hidden room. She couldn't make out exactly what they were, but chaos and violence spewed from every corner.

"Oh my god, Francis. What is this?"

Wenty pulled on Dot to describe what she saw.

Francis applauded her revelation, turning to face her with a tender eye. "It is what is, and what will be."

Dot noticed small illustrations toward the bottom of the walls, with lines shooting rays upward. *The goddamn dandelions*, she thought. Upon closer inspection, she could see markings of a girl in a chair with wheels and a boy with no eyes and a long stick. There was even a fat drawing of Archie with X's for ears. There were hills, flames, Blackburn's, rats, scissors, and a foreboding figure she could barely make out.

The unknown figure seemed huge and was draped in dark layers. Its head almost all beak— no—yes—and in its sack, tons of tiny images of what looked to be scissors.

"Who's that?" Dot said, pointing to the illustration.

"Mother."

"I don't understand what it is."

"Schnabelperchten."

"The Belly Slitter," Wenty whispered.

"*Quos Deus vult perdere, prius dementat*," Francis hissed.

"In fucking English, you twat," Dot snarled at the fire boy, sick of his games. "Why do they call it *The Belly Slitter*?"

"You'll know soon enough, Dorothy."

Francis walked over to his red-painted masterpiece and pointed to a crude drawing of a hill adorned with illustrated dandelions. "Here. This is where you will enact the ritual."

"And how do we do that?" Wenty interjected, wiping sweat from his forehead.

"Since time began," Francis said, pointing his nub finger to a drawing of the sun, "gods await mortals to ask of them. They are there to be wanted, needed. They desire to give. But they must first be . . . *enticed*," Francis said with a growing smile.

"I know this already," Wenty said, growing impatient with his parable-speak.

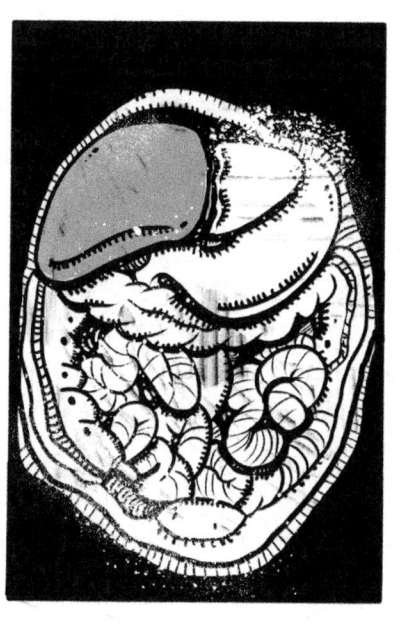

"Get on with the fairy tale horse shit!" Dot added her own eagerness. "Why in god's name is it a liver?"

Francis, unfazed, readied his posture as if waiting to be asked, as if he had rehearsed this moment before. "In the Prometheus myth, the ancients regarded the liver as a delicious organ, the capital of life." Francis shuffled to the corner of the boiler room, grabbing a large sheet of some kind, which swaddled something clunky, and dragged it to the table in front of them. Dot could tell it was heavy. She watched Francis return and grab a much smaller canvas school bag, stained in black, with sharp corners. The light in the boiler room danced as the flames raged, making the entire scene like a play. "It's the dwelling place of your soul."

"Fucking weird," Dot said, watching the fire boy.

"Your soul is like a shy animal. Only you can call it into the light."

"So we're offering her *our* liver-souls?" Wenty asked.

"No," Francis said, "you're offering her *a soul*."

"Who's?" Dot asked, pushing things along.

Then like a magician revealing his trick, Francis tore the sheet from the table and raised his arms, awaiting his own applause.

Dot immediately turned and threw up as Wenty covered his nose and mouth. The boiler room had sped up the decaying process, turning the partial corpse of Henry Bloomfield into soup and bones. Henry's corpse looked like it had been drained of all blood. It was then that she realized Francis's elaborate red wall paintings were done in her peer's blood. But before she could scream at Francis that he had gone too far, Francis opened the smaller canvas bag, arresting any emotions Dot could ever possess.

"No, no, no, not this way."

"What is it?" Wenty asked, afraid of knowing what she saw.

"It's Henry fucking Broomfield . . . It *was* Henry."

"You get one chance. You get one wish. You get one prayer. You get one offering," Francis interjected, raising his voice and squeezing the human meat. The sound of sludge and squish was deafening. "You both wish to be whole again, right?"

"Not like this!" Dot said with all the power she

could muster. But before she could continue her rant, Wenty grabbed her hand, "Please, Dorothy, I need to see you."

Dot, unable to help herself, started gagging. Francis grinned his satanic grin and opened the second bag. A plethora of cutlery that Francis had stolen from the kitchen and dining hall over the past few days sat jumbled together, reflecting the firelight.

Wenty waited for Dot to regain herself, but she continued vomiting onto her lap. He forced himself to step forward. He felt pulled, and he was sure it was love.

Wenty reached down and placed his soft hands on Henry's corpse, feeling and getting his bearings. He asked Francis for the sharpest knife he had.

Before Wenty entered the point of no return, he turned to Dot to gift her one final assurance. "If we go tonight, we can get this over with. Plus, no one will see us," he said with surprising peace. "Do you trust me?"

Dot agreed as the vomit dripped from her chin.

Remnant memories of Henry's voice flashed in Wenty's mind. The blind boy dropped the heavy steel blade on Henry's sternum hard and heard the snap. "Oh my god," the blind boy said. Francis applauded.

"Wenty," Dot said in terror behind her friend, her eyes moving back and forth between Wenty's dig and Francis's childlike nods of approval.

Wenty chopped and waved the blade like a shitty orchestral conductor. Blood splattered as he painted a masterpiece. "I can't," Wenty said defeatedly. "I just can't see what I'm doing . . ."

"Fuck it, let me do it," Dot said, taking the blade from Wenty's hands. Dot readjusted herself on the table next to Henry to be able to lift and swing. She had never held a blade this heavy, let alone brought it down upon something—or someone. But after she regained composure, she didn't hesitate and brought the blade down hard and fast. She split bones in two, making her own biblical red sea. Wenty covered his ears at the sound of chopping bones.

Then the search started. Full fists buried inside Henry as if he was a puppet. Dot's hand passed over, touched, and searched for anything that felt like a liver.

"Is this it?" she asked Francis, ripping the shriveling kidneys from Henry's open cavity. Francis gave a disapproving look. His stumpy hand was propped up, "shaking his head" at their findings.

Dot took a deep breath and put hands back inside Henry. She tried to remember anatomy class with Sister Carrie. She worked hard with her eyes closed to imagine the skeletal frame, the stomach . . . up . . . left. Dot knew she was done when she ripped out a grainy, toothy, pink sack and heard Francis's quick applause.

Dot brought the blade down again and again to release the liver from its fleshy leash. The room warmed the sinews, making them more like gum and glue. Francis raised his arms in submission and moved the sheet to a carrying tote, looking like a village butcher.

"Now the rest is up to you, and quickly. Morning will soon be upon us," Francis said, handing the liver to Dot without looking at her. His eyes fixed on the body. "Take his liver and bury it on the northern hill, the highest hill on the land, the one with the sycamore," Francis said, pointing to his painting of a tree. "Once you are there, bury the offering in the ground, and repeat three times what you wish for. It doesn't matter what time or how long it takes you. As long as you bury it in the earth. Then you wait."

Francis reached out with his bloody nub to pick Dot up, but she quickly stopped him. "Don't you touch me, you fuckstick," Dot said, recoiling.

Wenty helped Dot to the ground and dragged her up each stair, her boots thudding with each ascent as she did her best to help pull herself up with her arms. As they reached the top, Francis followed from behind, silhouetted by the fires of hell that was the boiler room.

Wenty remembered something as they were exiting the staircase. "Francis, you said you wished for purpose. What does that mean?" he asked, feeling the need to crush any remaining disbelief within himself.

"You are my purpose."

• • •

"Each day, this greedy vulture will tear open your body and gorge his voracious appetite upon your defenseless liver. Each night, your liver will regenerate itself to provide a renewed feast for the eagle on the following day. So consider my message, defiant Prometheus. Loud-thundering Zeus does not lie. His wishes become deeds. You can escape this agony only if some immortal, of his own free will, chooses to give up his own immortality and take your place in the depths of Tartarus. No matter how you twist and turn in the attempt to lessen your torture, just as you are handcuffed and staked to this cliff, so are you chained to your fate. As brilliant as you are, you cannot outwit the gods!"

PrometHeus

Every mile is two in winter.

—George Herbert

TWO CHILDREN TRAVERSED UP THE HILL with nothing to lose and everything to gain. Wenty pushed Dot's chair hard through the thick, crunchy snow. She was his vision, and he her legs. She his heart, and he her breath.

The dimming moon made it hard for Dot to see their trail, but she knew they were on the right path. Allowing her hand to droop, her fingers swayed between the soft dandelions. She could feel them blooming as Wentworth pushed determinedly up the hill. The dismembered pieces of a child they once knew lay on Dot's lap.

"Are we close? I'm not sure I can push much more through this snow."

"Not much further. *I think* . . . her words trailed off.

"You're not talking, so that means you're thinking."

"I am," Dot whispered.

"What, may I ask?"

"What do you think?"

"It's done, and soon we'll be free, Dorothy."

"Just because something ends, doesn't mean you stop living with it."

Wenty knew she was right, but he also knew a more glorious future could come.

"I mean, Jesus, Wentworth, I'm holding the liver of a dead kid on my lap, and we're going to bury it so some freaky god will come and grant us a wish. A wish to walk, a wish to see," Dot said, weeping between the words. "It doesn't feel right." Dot's hands massaged the sheet with Henry's liver as if apologizing to the dead boy. She stared at it. Then she noticed something that chilled her blood. The polka-dot sheet.

"It's not like we killed him; the rats did," Wenty whispered confidently. Pushing forward.

"Oh my god, Wentworth!" Dot shouted in distress.

"What? What is it!"

"It's Claire."

"What? What do you mean it's Claire!"

"Her sheet, her fucking polka-dot sheet!" Dot took the bundled bloody mess and turned it over in her hands, searching for confirmation of what she severely hoped was a coincidence. Then she saw it. A stained tag with the signed name of the baby she loved.

Wenty stopped pushing and held Dot steady to stop her from rolling backward down the hill and to steady her heart. It was all he could offer. No words could soften the tragic realization. But steadiness was something the boy could do. So he stood there in silent solidarity—torn between figuring out what to say and allowing silence to say it all.

After a few moments of silence, he continued his push, like Sisyphus rolling the boulder up the hill. But before Wenty could say anything, Dot grabbed his hand. He could feel it was different. Something was not right.

ARCHIBALD WAITED WITH PUCK on his shoulder for Dot and Wenty to leave the boiler room—a wait that felt like an eternity to the deaf boy. Archie could see they were carrying something bloodied and lumpy but paid no real attention to it as his focus shifted to the boiler room door. He saw Francis staring straight back at him from the blackness. Francis pulled his finger toward him, beckoning him.

"Go, my moonchild," Puck commanded in Archie's ear, forcing Archie to shuffle over to the entrance.

"I wondered where you've been. You haven't much time," Francis whispered through the cracked door, his voice echoing from the darkness.

Archie looked back in confusion at Francis's stiffened words. Puck pulled himself up to Archie's ear, translating Francis's words.

DOCTOR

"WUt iZ HappEnING? Wut R mY FrINZ DuINg?"

Francis offered his devilish grin and gently grabbed Archie's shirt, pulling him into the boiler room. "Come, let me show you."

• • •

He walked the perimeter of the building, counting the eye-level bricks as he went.

. . . 792, 793, 794, 795, 796 . . .

The snow smashed beneath his heavy boots as it reflected the moonlight, forcing it to glow a cerulean blue. The words repeated in his head rhythmically,

This is my house.

This is my house.

This is my house.

His voice, like a purring cat, was rhythmic and low. This is how he preferred to work—to assess with no tour. To see it with virgin eyes, the way new life would. The way a rat would. Small droppings hung from spider webs and speckled the snow. He looked up for its source; their hole-like eyes winked at him. He removed them one by one and placed them in the small glass jar that dangled from his neck.

This is my house.

He journaled quickly and often without looking, as if his hand was emancipated. He illustrated the school, its windows and arches, placing circles and x's where he noted entry points and circadian rat pathways. From his pack, he removed a large brass injection needle with a three-prong finger grip and a twenty-inch needle. He slid it slowly into every hole that felt right, a pleasure bordering on sexual for the doctor. He let out a guttural moan in his beak-shaped mask. He had penetrated the school over one hundred and fifty times with his own cocktail of rodenticide. His own metabolic disruption of anticoagulant, antibiotic, vitamin D, and botulinum toxin. One dose of this would bring nuclear disaster for any mischief or rat colony. Anything more than two or three could take down an entire circus, and anything beyond that could induce a genocide of all creatures living beneath the sun. *This is my house.*

● ● ●

Wenty could feel the hill leveling out, even though their conversation was escalating. There, before the two incomplete children on the northern hill beneath the sycamore tree, was a new world. It was as if their earth had a crack and other dimensions were leaking in. Infiltrating. Invading. A sinking feeling grew inside them like a Jupiter parasite, a worm in a honeycrisp, a tumor in the throat. It ate away any hope of security. Fear shot up their arms and down their spines. Wenty was growing familiar with this sense of apprehension; it was the same whenever Francis was around. "We're here. I know it," Wenty said.

"Oh my god, Wenty," Dot said through awe-struck whispers. "This can't be real."

The snow beneath them glowed with the colors of a wolf moon as millions of dandelions grew from the cold powder. As the wind blew their seeds into the winter air, it was impossible to tell what was snow and what was dandelion. The dandelions covered the children, getting in their mouths and hair, blocking out even the moonlight above. The kids couldn't be sure, but it felt like spring, the biting cold dissipating and heat radiating from the illuminating ground.

Dot looked farther to see the sycamore—its leaves were not blowing, more like bowing upward, a reverence of sorts. The tree was decorated in what looked like fruit, but even Dot knew that fruit didn't grow on sycamores, and as she stared harder, she could see it wasn't plums or apricots but hearts. Beating hearts hung like cocoons from their branches, pulsating and dancing in their suspension. Dot covered her mouth in a mixture of fear and revulsion. She would have gagged if she had anything left.

"What is happening?" Wenty asked. "What do you see?"

"Everything," Dot said. "Words cannot express where we're at, or *what* we're at. This isn't normal."

"What color is it?" Wenty asked again, needing something.

"All of them, and none of them."

"I don't understand. God, it feels warmer here, doesn't it?"

"Yeah," Dot said, looking upward, noticing through the dandelion storm that the stars above moved quicker, spinning even, as if the gods were twisting with earth.

"Let's get this over with," Wenty said, coming around and feeling for the liver on Dot's lap. "Here is as good a place as any, I guess," he said, kicking the ground beneath to make sure there weren't rocks or twigs hidden by the snow and dandelions.

Dot lowered herself from her chair and propped herself up in the bright snow, creating a puff of dandelions around her. The two children dug through the snow. The ground was surprisingly gentle and gave way easily with every scoop. The two children did not say a word.

"That's enough, Wenty," Dot said, seeing the hole was deep enough. As she stared into its dark pit, she realized it reminded her of a well. The kind she used to make childlike wishes in with her father before her accident—the kind of wish that harbored innocence and fantasies. Wenty tried to unwrap Broomfield's liver from Claire's disregarded bedsheet. Dot watched Claire's name flop around with Wenty's erratic movements. Then, with Henry's liver, and their wish, they rolled the organ out of its fabric coffin, allowing it to fall plumply into the so-called magical grave. Wenty reached for the liver, patting around for its whereabouts.

"God, Wenty!" she blurted in pain. "Claire. *My* Claire." She couldn't let her go.

"I know, I know. It's almost over. Stay with me, Dot. Soon we'll be safe and whole."

But something had moved within the girl who couldn't move. Dot, with her fierceness, looked at the blind boy with a disconcerting revelation. "But *they* won't be!" Dot said, wiping her eyes. "They—our friends, the children, the babies—will still be there in that cock-sucking rat maze! And we could have done something about it, but instead we're too fucking selfish and made a wish for just us. For fuck's sake, Archie could be hurt, or sick! God, he could be eaten!"

"But they said an exterminator is coming. We could have both," Wenty said, pleading with his love.

"They've had exterminators there a hundred times before, and look, I'm still holding a liver!"

Wenty was out of rebuttal. "So that's it? We wish for the rats to be gone, and I still go on blind, and you stay bound to this fucking chair?" Wenty said, raising his voice.

"At least we'll have each other, and we'll have saved those who can one day be rescued from that hell. I don't need to walk to be free. Do you need to see to be happy?" Dot said, gently laying the liver back in the hole. Dot continued, "I know what I'd wish for, but only if you wish it with me. We only get one shot at this. Will you wish this with me, Wentworth?"

The boy knelt before the hole, hands covered in filth, dandelions sticking to falling tears from unseeing eyes. His thoughts seized him in that moment for a thousand years as the severing of his dreams was lowered in that hole.

"Yes," he said through pained words.

Dot threw herself at her friend, forcing him to catch himself. He didn't immediately give in to the hug, as he could feel a seed of resentment toward the girl he loved, but once he heard her crying, he reached out his arms and brought her in close.

Dot began shoveling snow, dandelion weed, and soft dirt on top of the organ with vigor.

"Hurry, let's get this over with." And before long, the hole was filled. "Now what exactly do we do?" Dot asked.

"We wish."

"How?"

"I think it's like praying?" Wenty said, somewhat confused.

"I don't even know how to pray," Dot said, lying to herself. Dot knew from her countless gatherings with Father Gregory how to pray, how to worship, how to identify each Hellenistic letter between alpha and omega.

"I do. When you're blind, all you can do is pray," Wenty said, taking Dot's dirty hand in his. "We must come humbly but boldly. Confident that what we did was real. Then, we'll look down, close our eyes and say, 'We wish for these rats to be taken from this place.' How's that?"

Dot looked into his eyes. The bandage hid them, but she could see him beneath it.

"That's perfect, Wenty," she said with a smile.
"We wish for these rats to be taken from this place."
"We wish for these rats to be taken from this place."
"We wish for these rats to be taken from this place."

As the final prayer was spoken, Dot watched as every dandelion left the earth around them, soaring up to the cosmos—millions of fairies fleeing, gods stealing back their snow, a storm in reverse, the world turned upside down. The beating hearts shriveled, the stars stilled, and the air grew colder.

"We did it," Dot said, reaching into her night-gown pocket and retrieving her pipe. "Holy cock-balls, we fucking did it," she said, lighting it as she inhaled.

"This better fucking work."

THE DOCTOR PREFERRED TO WORK within the shadows. Lurking, humming, penetrating Blackburn's. The distant sound of children broke his focus. Two disabled children were holding something and making their way toward a distant hill. One had bandages on his eyes, pushing a young girl in a wooden wheelchair.

The doctor took out his pocket watch from his long coat—2:04 a.m. This brought a grin to his face as he wrote it down in his leather-bound journal. He watched the children until they were out of sight. But just as he was about to continue his work, another child, a much fatter one, opened the same door, following the other two children. He stalked more than followed them, like a predator to prey. The doctor shook his head, slightly amused by the situation, and reached for another jar to fill up his injector.

As he turned back to the building, his heart froze in fear. There, standing only a few feet away, was a little redheaded child, the night blocking most of the child's face and features. The plague doctor could tell something was terribly wrong with the boy.

"Hello, child?" He said through his mask, hiding his shock. The doctor watched as the little redheaded boy cocked his head to the side, the way a cat would to a dying robin. His face was in the dark from the shadows of the moon, but the doctor could see his hand was missing and his skin had been badly burned. Normally this would bring a prick of sympathy, but at two in the morning, it induced fear.

"What are you doing here?" Francis asked, sticking his finger on the tip of the plague doctor's injector needle.

"This is no place for a child," the doctor said, pulling back his instrument.

Francis drew his finger back, but only because he wanted to.

"Scurry on before I inform an adult."

"Do you think adults run this school?" Francis asked, coming into the moonlight. "Tell me, are you the one they call *the exterminator*?"

"I am," the doctor said with steadiness, unnerved by the child. There was something about the way he spoke, the way he moved. He didn't seem like a child. He seemed like something trying to *pretend* to be a small boy.

"And you think your poison will take the rats away?"

"No, I think it'll end them where they are. Listen, child, you must allow me to continue my work."

"What if *you* took the poison?"

The question brought chills down his spine, but the doctor couldn't figure out why. The doctor kept thinking to himself that this was some stupid kid, but he was unnerved between being unable to see his face, the stumpy hand, and the late hour.

"Little boy, I'm growing thin in patience with you—"

"Take some of the poison. I want to see," Francis interrupted.

"Now you're angering me."

In the distance, a young girl yelled, as if she was upset but not in danger. The doctor glanced at the northern hill, witnessing something he'd never expected. The hill was glowing, throbbing with light. He saw a flurry of snow blowing on top of the mountain. "What in god's name?" he whispered to himself as he turned back to the boy, only to see he was gone, leaving only the boy's footprints in the snow.

He followed the footprints with his eyes. Before vanishing, the boy had come extremely close to him without his knowledge and then turned around sharply. The thought made the doctor shudder. He regained composure, pleased to be left alone by the invalid. Going back to work, he reached for the last vial of poison he had on his belt, only to find it missing.

AS DOT AND WENTY CAME DOWN THE HILL, freezing and covered in dirt, they heard footsteps behind them. Wenty quickly lurched forward and flung the chair around.

"Archie?" Dot said in surprise.

Revealing himself like a vampire to the sun came the boy who couldn't hear.

"Jesus, Archie! Dude, where the hell have you been?" Wenty shouted, exasperated.

"It's pointless, Wenty. It's too dark for him to read our lips. Oh my god, Archie, what happened to you?" Dot could see that the plague had eaten away at the boy's face and body. "Oh my god, he's sick! Wenty, he's sick with the plague!"

Wenty took a step back in fear. "Archie, we need to get you help. Is this why you've been hiding?"

"wHy?!?" Archie asked, his old self breaking

through. "wWe MaDe A VOW!" His accusations spewed between guttural coughs, spraying the snow red beneath him. Dot and Wenty stood speechless as Archie showed them his palm and gestured to theirs. All three palms were face up, allowing the scarry slit of their purgatory pact to make its point.

"Archie . . ." Dot said with deep concern as she pulled her palm inward.

Before Wenty could roll Dot close enough, Archie marched toward the top of the hill.

"Archie?"

"Let him go," Dot said, pushing her chair herself.

"How can we? He's our brother, Dot!"

"Not anymore."

As Archie reached the flattened top of the hill, he looked for some sign or clue as to what his friends had done, but he was only met with the plain, white snow. It bleached the area, leaving no sign of what had just happened. Even their tracks were starting to be covered by the virgin snowfall.

Archie's blood boiled beneath his cold skin, but before he could actualize his rage, he spun his round body fast and hard, punching the sycamore tree but feeling nothing. The lack of pain brought pause to Archie's hunt for the buried treasure. Archibald's swollen, bulbous hands spurted pus and blood from the impact, bringing Archie to his knees in shock. His other hand grasped his throat and heart while his body struggled to breathe. The plague moved inward, laying its eggs within himself, suffocating the boy who couldn't hear.

Archie frantically searched for their offering, burying both hands in the snow. Desperate to find the location of their betrayal, he lay prostrate in the reddening snow, the ice cooling his globose frame, quickly creating a small mound of snow and dirt. "I FOAwND iTT!" he shouted to Puck.

The rat scurried to where his bloodied, lumpy hands dug.

Archie slowed his mission, waiting for his wish to finally be granted now that his perceived bidding was complete.

"MAke mE heAAr! MaKe Me heAr! MAKe me norMAAALL! SAuVe mE!" He was weeping and angry, his light quickly fading as slop streamed down his face. He could no longer get breath in his lungs through the eggy knobs in his throat. He was drowning in his own pustules. With a dying breath, he reached hard for Puck, his love, "HeLP meeeeeeee!"

Puck's calm, indifferent gaze was matched by a tail at peace. He watched from a distance as his moonchild sailed upon the river Styx, entering the open gates of death. Nodding, accepting, encouraging eternity's portion, Puck's final words echoed to the boy who once lived . . .

"Moonchild, you will be saved, but not through wishes, only through suffering."

THE FATHER REACHED INSIDE THE MOTHER, pulling and tugging on the child stuck within her. At times, he couldn't tell if he was grabbing a part of the mother or the child clinging to her. His large arms stretched the mother's dilation to degrees no woman could withstand, and soon the mother faded into blackness from the pain. This brought joy to the father, as her screams were beginning to hurt his ears.

Finally, the father got a full grip on the infant's head and dragged it out of the warm tunnel. He slipped a few times from the slime, causing him to spit his cigarette out of his mouth and focus. Then, finally, the baby came, falling to the floor like a wild animal, purple and blue.

"Jesus Christ," the father said with great annoyance as he eyed his wife to see if she awakened from the thump of her baby's head. A knock at the rickety door pulled his attention to his other children. Six of the nine came in, hoping to catch a glimpse of their new sibling and check on their mother's well-being.

"Get!" the father shouted, wiping his hands with his wife's nightgown and lighting another cigarette.

"Should I pick the boy up?" his eldest daughter asked.

"I said, get!"

The new infant lay motionless. God only knew if it was dead or not.

"Father?" the eldest daughter again. This time it invited a backhand.

"God dammit, let me handle this! Go and watch your siblings."

The father picked up his tenth child and examined it. He cut cords and removed slime from its eyes and genitals. To his own shock, he was relieved it passed on—a stillborn.

In a moment of reprieve, the father tossed the baby into a steel bucket beside the nightstand and turned his attention to the unconscious mother. But as the baby boy hit the steel, like Lazarus, it came back. Screaming and moaning echoed from the cold bucket, and where a right father would find joy, he felt dread. His relief of losing a mouth to feed was greater than the joy of having another child to love, forcing him to move quickly before the other children heard the baby's cries.

Leaving through the bedroom's back door, he swiftly made his way with the bucket to the pond behind the small, dilapidated home. There, he filled it with river rock and pebbles. In a single motion, he tossed it in the middle of the mossy water.

Breathing heavily but confident in his decision, he returned to tell his children that their baby brother had gone to be with God. He had no idea that his eldest daughter had also slipped through the back door. She hid and watched behind the skeletal trees. Once her father had made it back inside, she removed her shoes and dove into the green pond, retrieving her brother, who sat at the bottom waiting for her for many, many, many long minutes.

Knowing her father would find rage in her rescuing the infant and that she herself was far too young to raise a child, she did the only thing she could: take him to Blackburn's Catholic Boarding School & Orphanage. Beneath the twilight, she followed the train tracks to the school.

She ran until her chest throbbed painfully, the baby in her arms, sleeping beside her rapid heart. Then she noticed something disturbing, something unnatural. As she waited for the loud midnight train to pass, preparing for the child to awaken with screams, she saw no stirring or motion . . . only peace, as if he was unbothered by the screeching noises or hadn't heard them at all.

Arriving at the school's stone steps, she removed her headcover and swaddled the child tight, scribbling on a sliver of paper the child's name, a name that meant bravery and boldness. A name her grandfather once possessed. There she placed the deaf infant and the note, kissed the top of his purpled soft head, and whispered, "Forgive us, Archibald."

● ● ●

The following morning after the wish had been made, Dot and Wenty sat in the food hall digging through their runny eggs. Memories of shoveling dirt moved in and out of their minds like passing ghosts as they scraped their food. Each of their hands was still caked in the remnants of a night in hell.

"Is it done?" Francis asked, dropping his pewter food tray loudly on the table.

"Yes," Dot said, raising her eyes to meet his lifeless ones.

Wenty, not even looking up, felt deflated after last night's decision. Feelings of regret stabbed him.

"How long 'til it happens?" Dot asked.

"The earth must spin one time."

"So tonight?" Wenty asked. "Just say 'tonight,' ass-goblin. Holy fuck."

"Did the fat one join you in the wish?"

"No," Dot said through grieving words.

Francis's shark-like eyes shot up in concern. "He must have. I promised three."

"You promised three what?"

Francis rocketed up from his chair, leaving his food. He looked around for a sign of Archie, Dot assumed. "What's going on? Three *what*, Francis?"

The fire boy marched off as quickly as he came, ignoring her questioning.

"God, he's just the worst!"

Wenty no longer wanted to hear Dot's self-righteous opinion. "You know what?" Wenty shouted.

"*Ssshhh*, you're yelling, dude!"

"Fuck, Dot," Wenty said, shaking his hands as if gripping her neck.

"What's gotten into you?"

"I'll tell you! It's how everything you think or do is the only path. And if we don't walk that path, or Francis doesn't walk it, we're all mamby bamby's!"

"What is happening?"

"We had our chance, and now it's fucking gone!"

Dot came to a realization, placing her face in her hands. "You agreed that protecting these kids was the better choice! I didn't force you to make that wish."

"No, you're right. You didn't force me. But you certainly gave me no other option." Wenty slammed his fist on the table and stood up with his cane, making his exit, leaving the girl alone to realize that her only family was slowly being sawn asunder.

The world? Moonlit
Drops shaken
From the crane's bill.

—**Dogen (1200–1253)**

"DOT, WAKE UP," Wenty spoke through a forced whisper.

"What do you want?"

"Can you hear it?" Wenty asked, his voice almost inaudible.

Beyond the northern hill was a low-frequency chant, almost a vibration, just on the threshold of human hearing, like the bleating of lambs to a slaughter. It wasn't particularly loud. In fact, one wouldn't even notice it—but once you did, you couldn't stop hearing it. The blind boy with deft ears was first to hear it and sat up in his bed as the noise rumbled above the sleeping children's hums.

"Fuck me, what is that?" Wenty asked again.

"What? I don't hear it," Dot shot back, rolling her useless legs over to the other side. The heavenly feeling of the cool side of the bed sheets against hot legs was lost on her.

Wenty stood from his bed and pressed his ear against the painfully cold winter glass. "That sound, oh my god, that sound."

"You don't think it's . . ." Dot suggested. She sat up and pushed away the curtains from the windows between the two of them. Orange moonlight streamed in, painting the room a different dimension. She could see through the harvest light that Wenty was breathing erratically. His chest tightened as the chanting faded in and out, coming and going in the darkness as if the moon had a heartbeat. "Calm down, Wentworth. I'm sure it's nothing," she said as the mysterious clangor grew louder and shook the snow off the glass windows, causing Wenty to whimper in fear. Dot continued scouring the other slumbering children. None seemed bothered by the growing noise. "I don't think anyone can hear it—"

"You don't think she's here, do you?" Wenty asked, interrupting Dot's realization.

"The Belly Slitter?"

"Is this it? Is our wish being granted?" Wenty asked back.

"Wait, I just thought the rats would disappear.

I don't understand the noise. What do you hear exactly?"

"Ga ga ga . . ." Francis said, standing directly behind the two children, bathed in tangerine light.

"Geez, Francis, how the hell . . .?" Dot said, placing her hand over her heart.

"Oh, foolish ones, it's not noise," Francis said.

"What is it then?" Dot asked.

"It's her hymn, a spiritual song, a harmony in fire. This is how she grants your wantings."

"It's getting louder," Wenty said anxiously.

"It sounds like chanting," Dot asked, knowing Francis had answers he wasn't sharing.

"Ga ga ga . . ." Francis choked out through his teeth, his eyes never leaving the hills that slept beyond the school's borders.

"What happens now? Are the rats gone?" Dot asked, pulling herself into her chair, fully awake now.

"What's going on?" Giggy asked from the corner.

"Get your ass back in bed, you barf-nugget!" Dot burst at the fat boy.

"I swear, Giggy, if I hear so much as a butt burp come from your direction, I'll turn your ass into butter!" Wenty joined in the shaming.

"Ga ga ga . . ." Francis said again.

Wenty understood now. He could hear those words as a chorus over the neighboring hills. He placed his hands over his mouth in fear. This was larger than what he could have imagined. What had they awakened? "Francis, tell us now what we should be expecting!"

Dot turned to face the fire boy, but before she could smack sense into his nonsensical ranting, she heard it. Her ears pricked to a chorus of quaking and squeals, a familiar sound and smell she'd heard streaming through these walls before, but this time it felt as if it were growing to its climax.

"Oh my god," Dot said, shoving Wentworth back onto his bed. She lifted her legs and folded them in her lap at the same moment a panic of rats broke in from every crevice. She watched as Francis stood there among the rats, raising his arms as if he was nailed to a ghostly crucifix and looking up toward the heavens. The sleeping children began waking, screaming, their cries lost to the squeaks of the vermin crawling upon them.

Using the children and their beds as bridges to the windows, the rats crashed through the glass, freeing themselves into the winter night. Each one a different shade of energy beneath orange light, they made their way toward the hill, the source of the sound.

Wenty bit down hard on his lip as he screamed in terror, drawing blood beneath his blankets. The event didn't stop for what felt like hours, tiny feet punching and groping the terrified children beneath them, rat tails whipping their skin and face.

The school's staff appeared at the doors, torches in hand, only to be met with shock as rats rivered themselves through their legs and thighs, unencumbered by their presence. They tried to shout words of authority, but that too was lost in the panic.

And then, just as it began . . . it was over.

The remaining rats lifted themselves to the windowsill and jumped to the snow below, leaving the children and their vermin-less home in silence.

"Children!" Sister Margaret called out.

One by one, the children poked their heads from their blankets like moles from the earth. Hair and tiny specks of shit peppered the beds. A constellation of feces was all that was left of the harrowing affair.

A few of the beds had rats that had been flattened by the stampede; others had yellow and red stains.

"What just happened?" a young girl yelled out. Soon, all the children chattered in relief and wonderment.

"Quiet. Quiet down," Sister Margaret rebuked. "I think they're gone . . . " She placed her ear against the walls with a prayer for silence. "Yes, yes, yes . . . I don't hear anything. The exterminator did it!"

The children followed suit, placing their ears against the stone walls. Dot looked swiftly at Wenty to see his reaction to Sister Maragret's cry and smiled. They were saved, and their doings were hidden from the world. They did it. They created a haven.

The children shouted with joy, the first time Dot or Wenty had heard this type of noise within these walls. Dot even found herself giggling. Wenty too was starting to smile as he wiped the blood from his chin and cheeks. She looked toward Archie's bed.

He lay flat, blankets pulled over his head like a corpse, unmoving. She watched long enough to make sure he was breathing, noting there was no celebration from his bed. She knew then what had happened . . . *Oh god, Puck*, she thought.

As she flipped the blanket back from his from fabric cocoon to offer comfort, she discovered a false body made of pillows and clothes. *Where the fuck is Archie?*

PART TWO

THE FOLLOWING MORNING, the school staff and clergy allowed the children to sleep in late, ensuring the school bell was turned off. After the night they'd had, they deserved a little reprieve. Heavy blankets were nailed to the windows after the rats bashed themselves through them in an attempt to keep out the cold. Despite the sleeping corridor's chilly temperature, the children were hot with excitement thanks to the realization that the rats were gone for good.

Dot awoke for the first time with a smile, hopeful and present to the other children surrounding her, the children she had saved. From her pillow, she could smell breakfast brewing in the dining hall—sugar and soft bread.

"Pancakes?" Wenty asked through a groggy voice as if reading Dot's mind.

"I think so!"

"Wow, that's a first."

"Today will be a day of firsts, Wenty."

She watched as Wenty formed a smile. She knew he was saddened by their decision not to be whole, but she also knew he'd come around to their right and moral decision. *A decision heroes make*, she thought. Dot propped herself up further to see if Archbald was in bed, and like most mornings these days, he was not.

"Don't worry. He's probably in the cafeteria already," Wenty said through a yawn.

"Maybe. We need to find him. To help him. He's sick."

"Agreed," Wenty said, sitting up finally. "We should tell Sister Margaret as soon as we can."

Wenty held onto Dot's chair as they made their way to the dining hall. They saw the school staff standing in a row, waiting for the children. They were met with smiles and relief, applauding the children as they made their way in for breakfast.

"Welcome, Dorothy," Sister Carrie exclaimed.

"Good morning."

"*Great* morning," Sister Teresa shouted in the back.

"So, is it real? Are they actually all gone?" a child asked.

"As far as we can tell. The extermination worked!"

"When was the extermination?" Wenty asked.

"We had an exterminator here late last night, fumigating the property, and whatever he did was successful."

"He was here *last night*?" Dot said, grabbing Wenty's arm.

"Yes, he needed to work at night knowing all of the rats would be huddled in a single space and to make sure no children would interrupt his work."

"Now what?" Dot asked. "Do you think the night mother might return now that the rats are gone?"

"Unsure, but for us . . . We go on!" the nun proclaimed.

The other children slowly marched into the room, their cheeks cold from their slumber but their eyes alive.

"Eat, children, eat!" Father Gregory shouted with joy, making his way to Dorothy. "How are you this morning, child?" he asked with relieved eyes.

Dorothy smiled to pacify the moment. The priest's presence always made her more emotional than she liked.

"Dorothy, can I have a word?" Sister Margaret asked. "How is Archibald? I know he had a pet rat," the nun said, pushing the invalid's chair through the food line and assisting her with her breakfast.

"You know about Puck the Rat?"

"Of course! We're not all ignorant. It's our job to know the students, and Archibald loved that damn rat. We never had the heart to take that one. It seemed harmless."

"It was, but I haven't seen him or his rat."

"Hmm," the nun moaned. "Do keep an eye out for him."

Dot nodded, knowing that was all she'd ever done. "I do need to talk to you, Sister. It's quite important."

But as Dot was about to explain Archie's condition, Sister Teresa burst into song at the other end of the hall, and soon the children and staff joined the chorus. Children were singing, not out of command, but out of contentedness. The cafeteria in concert raised their voices to the God above in praise. Sister

Margaret sang loudly, then made a determined walk to the entrance of the school. Dot could see a woman across the way waving at the nun, beckoning her.

Holy, holy, holy! Lord God Almighty!
Early in the morning, our song shall rise to thee;

Holy, Holy, Holy! merciful and mighty,
God in three persons, blessed Trinity!

Holy, holy, holy! All the saints adore thee,
casting down their golden crowns around the
glassy sea;
cherubim and seraphim falling down before thee,
who were and art and evermore shalt be.

All creatures of our God and King,
lift up your voice and with us sing
Alleluia! Alleluia!

Thou burning sun with golden beam,
thou silver moon with softer gleam,
O praise Him, O praise Him!
Alleluia! Alleluia! Alleluia!

Wenty too joined in song, clapping his hands together like a traveling evangelist. Dot worked hard to relax and tried to join in, but she couldn't. This surprised her, as she had a hidden hope that this ordeal would conjure a spirit that wasn't there before. She even tried to mouth the words, but her heart wouldn't let her. She felt as if an invisible grip held her throat. Despite the victory, she felt like a bird in a cage, and she wasn't sure why.

DURING BREAKFAST, a subtle knock sounded at the school's door. The singing and chatter were so loud that the individual decided to let themselves and their baggage in. The woman made her way to the concerto of children's voices with a package in hand, holding it close to her breast, as if it was the only thing on this earth that mattered. There, she finally spotted Sister Margaret, the only staff she knew, and waved her over, the preoccupied children left unaware.

"Hello, Rosemary! What a joy to see you!" the nun cried. "The exterminator did it, and we're elated."

"The exterminator did it?" the secretary asked. "You mean the rats have been killed?"

"More like surrendered the school to us," the nun corrected.

"What do you mean?"

The nun's face quickly changed disposition, seeing Rosemary's confusion. Sister Margaret's gaze shifted to whatever Rosemary was holding. "What do you have there, Rosemary?"

"In a moment. Are you saying the rats left?"

"Yes, at a late hour last night. After the exterminator had finished."

"That's . . . impossible," Rosemary said, darting her eyes to the floor. Confusion plagued her face.

"Why is that?"

"Well, for starters, the doctor said it would take days or even weeks due to the quantity of the infestation. On top of that, rats don't leave after an extermination. They die in place."

"Well, I don't know what to tell you," Sister Margaret said, "we have smart vermin." She offered a smirk.

"I guess so," Rosemary added. "Either way, I'm not here in matters of extermination. I'm here to give you . . . *her.*"

"Her?"

"This baby."

The nun looked down as Rosemary gently passed the child to her. "Ah, I see. That's Claire," the nun observed. The secretary's bandaged hands gave pause to the nun. "Are you okay, Rosemary? Your hands . . . my goodness."

Once the nun took the child, Rosemary recoiled and quickly tried to recover a sense of normalcy. "I'm fine, just a small mistake."

The nun sensed something was off and leaned in, embracing the young secretary. Rosemary pulled away. "I just thought the child should have a proper burial, with people who knew her."

"Thank you, Rosemary. I suppose you're right. She did save us, you know." the nun added.

Rosemary pressed her lips together, nodded, and turned to exit the school. "Oh, one more thing, Sister."

"Yes?"

"The sickness is spreading, so please keep the children safe."

"Absolutely. Everyone here is safe and sound," the nun insisted.

"DID YOU TALK TO SISTER MARGARET about Archie's condition?" Wenty asked through a mouthful of breakfast cake.

"Not yet. She sort of ran off," Dot said, poking at her food.

"Well shit, let's go talk to her before it's too late."

He's right, Dot thought. *Enough pissing around. Archie was out there dying, becoming less of himself, changing.* And Dot was growing selfish, jaded in her attempts to help him.

"He doesn't want our help."

"Fuck's sake, Dot! What happened to you?" Wenty shouted.

"You were hellbent on saving everyone here, and now you've grown soft?" Wenty said, taking another bite. "Archie is our friend. Let's help him, now!"

"You're right, let's go," Dot said, wheeling out

of the food hall. She found Sister Margaret closing the massive old school doors, holding something close to herself. "Sister, we need to talk," Dot said confidently.

Alarmed by the sudden presence, the nun instinctively held the cargo close to her chest. "Not now, Dorothy. I've got more important things at the moment."

"No I don't think—Is that . . . a baby?" Dot said, peering at the familiar shape of the parcel.

The nun was at a loss for words, knowing how intimately Dot cared for this child. "Dorothy, my highest recommendation would be to get back to breakfast."

"Wait, is that Clarie?" Dot asked with growing intensity.

"Oh, god," Wenty whispered to himself.

"Dorothy, now is most definitely not the time. I need to get this . . ." The sister was at a loss for words as to what to call the thing in her arms. A corpse? A baby? Then with gained composure, she said, "I need to get this baby to the boiler room as soon as I can. Before the other children see her . . . it."

Dot looked at Wenty, knowing what lurked in the boiler room. Allowing her full emotion to take over, she pleaded, "No! You can't!"

"Why is that?"

"Let me. She was my responsibility. Allow me to have these final moments with her. Some closure."

"Dorothy, there is no way—"

"Archibald has the plague!" Wenty exploded.

"What?"

Dot's eyes grew as large as potpies in Wenty's direction.

"How do you know this?" the nun asked.

"Dot saw him last night. Something was really wrong. He's got boils and growths all over the place. We're scared for him," Wenty added.

"Oh my god, we need to shut this school down now!" the sister thundered, frightened for her own life and the life of every child under her wing. "Here, Dorothy, take Clarie to the boiler room and then find me immediately. I need to find Father Gregory." Against her better judgment, she placed the corpse gingerly on Dot's lap. "Oh, and for God's sake, do. Not. Look. At. Her. Do you understand me? You

will not be able to handle it," the nun's final words
hit like a bolt of electricity. Then, like a cockroach
in the light, the nun scurried away, leaving the two
of them with the dead infant.

"ONE THOUSAND POUNDS, and not a penny less," the plague doctor said, not removing his beaked mask after the mayor had politely urged him to. The mayor's curiosity was piqued.

"Not a chance," the mayor said, spinning the golden rings on his fingers. "Listen, we're grateful for what you've done, but we can't afford that."

"What can you afford?"

"Are we negotiating now?"

"No," the doctor said, shifting himself. The movement from his leathery uniform was loud as the hide rubbed against itself. "I'm seeing how much I will have to take from you that lies beyond schillings."

"Is that a threat, *doctor*?" the mayor jabbed, deepening his already low voice.

The plague doctor tilted his head, studying the mayor behind round glass eyes. He always thought about his words carefully before sharing them. "I don't deal in threats, only absolutes."

Entering from the cold, Rosemary approached the mayor's study and pressed her ear against the large wooden door. Something she often did. She was surprised to be met with muffles. She removed her jacket, dusted the snow off her boots, and quickly checked the mayor's schedule on her desk, noticing that no one was scheduled to meet with him.

"I fear for you," the plague doctor said rebukingly.

"Don't. I live a good life."

"That is my fear, mayor. You value only that which can be taken."

"And what do you value?"

"What no one can take . . ."

"I think we've had enough for today. The best we can do is fifty pounds . . . *and not a shilling more,*" the mayor repeated, retrieving a small sack from his desk drawer and tossing it on the plague doctor's lap.

"One thousand pounds."

"Fifty."

"I will give you one more chance."

The mayor stood up to tower over the doctor, asserting his dominance. It was just short of pissing on him like a street dog. "Get the fuck out of here before I call the authorities."

The doctor stood, gently laying the money back on the table.

"I'll be in touch, Mr. Mayor," the doctor said as he left the office, quietly shutting the door behind himself.

"Thank you again," Rosemary said upon seeing the doctor leave. "For the rats, that is."

The doctor's only response was acknowledging her presence, not her opinion.

"Can I ask you something before you leave?" Rosemary asked.

Without replying, the doctor stopped and stared, giving Rosemary the moment.

"How is it possible that the poison worked so quickly? When we had spoken, you informed me it could take days or even weeks for a full termination."

"It's not possible."

"So then how did—"

"Do you have a receipt for my work?" the doctor asked. "The mayor promised a written form documenting my labor."

Rosemary, surprised by the ask, shook her head slightly. "I can write one for you if you'd like."

"Very much so."

Rosemary got up from her office chair and motioned toward the hall. "Give me just a moment to grab the documents."

The doctor lifted the lock latch on each window in the office and made his exit, abandoning both Rosemary and the receipt. He gave one final look at the windows and jotted a few notes down in his journal. *Two hundred in square footage, fourteen to fifteen hundred bricks, six windows.*

"FATHER GREGORY, can I have a word with you? It's quite urgent."

"Of course, Sister. What is it?" the priest said, sipping his tea.

"I have . . . upsetting news." The priest lowered his cup, feeling the room's energy shift with the tone of her voice.

"Dorothy and Wentworth have just informed me that they believe Archibald carries the plague."

"Oh lord, his rat."

"My thoughts exactly."

"Where is he now?"

"That's the problem. No one can find him."

"Stop whatever it is you're doing, gather the others, and search the premises," the priest said, wrapping a scarf around his neck to prepare for the search.

"And then what?" the nun asked with foresight.

"I . . . I'm not sure," the priest said, taking one final sip of his warm tea. "God grant us wisdom."

"Amen," the nun said, making the sign of the cross.

"But, for heaven's sake, do not touch him if you find him."

"I'm terrified, Father."

The priest took the nun in his arms. "Be not afraid nor dismayed, for the Lord goes before you in all that you do." The nun nodded and wiped the tears from her eyes. "You and the sisters start inside. I'll do an outside perimeter check and walk the fence line starting with the northern hill."

"Be careful," the sister cautioned.

● ● ●

Wenty kept a sturdy grip on the handrail and another on the dead baby which dangled from his arms. Every step was another stride toward what lay in wait inside the boiler room. His only light was the increasing heat from the inferno that called to him from below.

"You're doing great, Wenty. Keep going!" Dot yelled at the top of the stairs from her chair. Soon the blind boy would be out of sight as the stone stairs began their twisting descent.

"I can do this. I can do this. I can do this," Wenty whispered to himself, slowly lowering every footfall on the crooked stones. He continued until there was nothing left to lower upon.

In the cosmic blackness lay a vast open space. With no cane to poke around or help orient himself, Wenty wanted to drop the corpse and make his way back to Dot, but she made him promise he'd carefully lay Clarie upon a table to be found easily by the nuns. Using his right arm as a makeshift staff, Wenty felt his way around, groping through the thick darkness in search of anything solid.

Canvas

Wood

Steel

Hot

Cold

His feet kicked objects between steps.

Then he heard something. Giggling. The blind boy stopped to listen, knowing he was on full display like a marionette in the town square. He strained to hear as blood was pushed to his ears with the effort, forcing them to be better than they were. Embers popping and the furnace moaning concerted themselves in the forefront, masking whatever he thought he heard. Finally, he found a surface large enough to lay a baby upon. And there he laid the child, doing his best to lay its swaddled clothes over its eyes and cheeks.

"I'm sorry, Claire," he whispered to the nothingness of the boiler room, hoping she would hear his prayer in heaven.

Another childlike giggle from the corner of the boiler room gave Wenty gooseflesh, forcing him to abandon the ordeal and run toward where he remembered the stairs to be, tripping over objects. As he crawled up the stairs like an animal on all fours, he was almost certain he heard a small rapid applause as he made his exit.

● ● ●

The priest narrowed his eyes in the blinding white snow, shading them to scour the Lord's property for the missing child. If anything, he was almost grateful for the purity of the snow, as it allowed him to see a child playing, running, or hiding more clearly.

"Archibald!" the priest shouted here and there, only to be met with winter bird calls and icy wind.

Becoming out of breath at the top of the hill reminded the priest of his age. As he struggled to regain composure, he noticed an unusual disturbance. What was once a flat plain now had bumps and lumps scattered under a thick layer of snow. The sycamore tree he had spent years admiring and sitting under while laughing with the children as he read stories like Zacchaeus of Luke nineteen was covered in a splatter of crimson blood. The priest shielded his mouth in fear, and as he came closer for further inspection, he kicked something soft beneath the white sheet of snow.

It was then he knew he had found another dead child at Blackburn's.

• • •

"It's done!" Wenty said, sweaty and out of breath.

"What happened down there? Why are you so out of breath?" Dot asked, grabbing Wenty's hand for stability.

Wenty could not let his newfound reputation move backward in Dot's eyes, so he lied to protect his pride. "It was nothing. Just a long hike back up."

"Okay," Dot said with a hint of skepticism, "Claire's body okay?"

"On the table, just as you requested."

"Thank you, Wentworth," Dot said, giving his hand one final squeeze. "But like you said, we need to find Archie as soon as possible."

Wentworth took one final deep breath to calm his heart, snagged his cane from Dot, and gave an affirming nod. "I'm sure he's fine. If there is anything we know about that dude, he's a survivor."

• • •

The priest wrapped his winter jacket around the plagued child to not only protect himself but also avoid looking at the disturbed body. The bubonic disease did not stop at death, nor did the cold slow its momentum.

Archie's eyes were so pressed together by the batches of disease lumped on his forehead and nose that only slits remained—small cracks where once lay large, brown eyes. His ears were like gourds, and his coloring was gray. The priest could barely lift the portly child in his old age, his body had gone into full frozen rigor mortis which made it unusually uncomfortable to maneuver the corpse.

A tearing sound made itself heard as the priest unearthed Archie from his frozen coffin. All the while, the priest prayed and gagged. Only his tears kept him warm as he methodically brought the boy inside. As he passed Purgatory, he remembered how special it was for the child. He passed by the stained glass visuals of past titans reaching new heights while feeling like his life was sinking. "It's okay, my son," he continued to mumble to the boy whose laughter and youthful energy once ran through these halls.

"Oh my, oh my, oh my," Sister Margaret cried while coming around with the other staff trying to help hold the child.

"Stay back!" the priest said authoritatively.

The sisters cried and held each other at the sight of another dead child they knew and loved.

"The boiler room?" Sister Margaret asked.

"The boiler room," the priest confirmed.

"I'll call the coroner. We'll see if he's willing to come now since the rats have been terminated," Sister Carrie announced. "Thank you, Sister," the father said.

As Margaret opened the door for the priest, he made his way into the narrow, darkened corridor. "Be sure no one—and I mean no one—tells Dorothy or Wentworth about this until I speak with them. Do you understand?"

The nuns nodded in unison like seabirds and shut the door behind him, leaving him alone once more on his pilgrimage to hell with another lost soul.

CENTURIES BEFORE THE PLAGUE placed its print upon the world, there lived a handsome man. A man so handsome even the sun would blush at his doting presence. He was a hero, a man on a mission, a champion of lightning and stars. And as the world bowed to his beauty and strength, one particular creature knew what he really was. A black swan.

This creature, far more beautiful and enhanced than the hero, paid special attention not to the hero's accomplishments, but to his potential. His future held more stars than his past. The swan didn't bow to him, squawk praise, or lavish in his presence like the others, and it consumed the hero. So one day, when the earth was night, the hero sought to capture this black swan, but in his attempt he died by the icy waters and his sculpted body rose to the rocky shore. Each piece of him like marble burst and boomed amongst the watery floor, forcing his remains to scatter. His mother, who loved him more than she should, came one night, gathered each of the fingers, toes, elbows and bones, and sewed them back together.

But sadly, this did not bring her son back to life.

Not until she sent an orchid bee to fetch a bit of the god's honey. Then, upon the bee entering Lemminkäinen's mouth and flying to his heart, did he return from the underworld and claim his throne as twice-born.

LEMMINKÄINEN

THE PRIEST LAID THE BOY TO REST on one of the tables in the boiler room, the way Lazarus was cocooned in his stone. Father Gregory quickly recited a broken prayer and retreated to tend to his other duties.

After a while, the furnace heat softened Archibald's hard body. Stiff joints loosened, organs let themselves go, and bones became soft. Archie's bulbous face turned pliable from the heat, forcing the sores to pop and ooze down his cheeks, thighs, and pits. If one was quiet enough, one could hear each of the bulbs squirt and spray.

Then, from somewhere within Archie, something squirmed. A small wrinkle formed, followed by something in his stomach making itself known. From the pocket of his overalls, Puck emerged. He perched on top of the dead boy, warming his whiskers and tail by the furnace fire.

Puck scurried to the boy's knees to lick, then to his toes with a lick, and finally back up to his brow with another lick. It was as if he was checking to make sure everything was intact. Once Archie's mouth was warm enough to pry open and the proper time had passed, with his sharp, yellowed teeth, Puck pulled on Archie's infected bottom lip, opening the black hole that was his mouth. Puck gave a final twitch of his whiskers and went nose-first into Archie's mouth. If one didn't know better, it would have looked like Archie sucked him in like a noodle.

It took Puck a few tries to shift the fat tongue out of the way of Archie's throat, like removing a biblical stone from the messiah's grave in the garden. But with gentle sways and a few tugs, Puck was victorious. Sliding and cascading through the boy's esophagus, through the stomach to the center of his being—the liver. The delicious golden liver, its texture like that of Atlantic sand. Puck knew exactly where it was, and even if he didn't, the rich, musty smell of urine and dimethyl disulfide guided him to it like a far-off lantern at midnight. The rat entered the liver the way a newborn enters our galaxy, nestled and content in the dead child like a bee in honey.

Hopeful.

Tightly.

Worriless.

Determined.

Then, after a few moments of internal settling, as the furnace continued to rage, something unexplainable happened deep within Blackburn's. A cosmic stirring. A fleshy eclipse. A most terrible metempsychosis.

Archibald opened his eyes.

TRANSFIGURATION

LOW, RHYTHMIC SCRATCHING SOUNDS pulled the boy from his eternal slumber. The noise irritated Archibald as it itched his ears like insect bites. Subconsciously, he pounded his lumpy, diseased ears, jamming his filthy fingers deep within them to stop the wretched noise. *The fucking noise won't stop.* Archie thought to himself. *Make it stop!*

Pulling his finger from his ear, he could see fresh pink blood from penetrating too deeply.

I can hear?

Fire crackles, giggles, exhaust valves, heartbeats, shuffles, scurries, blood flow, children shouting and playing above, and then . . . a small voice.

"Can you hear me?"

"Who's there?" Archie asked, hearing his own voice for the first time, grabbing his throat in shock. The pain of it, the shock of it, brought tears to his eyes.

"I am."

"Puck?"

"Yes, Moonchild."

"Where are you? Oh god, where are you?"

"I'm here, within you, closer to you than your own breath."

"I don't understand . . ."

"Close your eyes. Do you see me?"

Archie did as he was told and closed his slitted, diseased eyes. Before him was a cosmological dance. Neptunic blue light broke through the nebula wind and dashed from side to side. "I see you."

"Now we are one, just as promised."

"But what about us being together?"

"We are more than together. We are one. A unison more tightly bound than color. You orbit me, and I pull for you."

"Wait, wait, wait!" Archie screamed, sweating from the flames before him. "I saw the rats leave. How are you here? Why weren't you taken with the others?" Archie continued his turmoil, pulling at his skin, trying to take it apart to free the rat within until he heard the worst words one could have spoken to the resurrected child . . .

"I was taken with them."

Archie's eye fixated on the flames, his arms coming to a halt, dropping like an ape's to his sides.

Spit and tears pushed through his eggy face lumps and rained upon the hot stone floor.

"Do you see it now?" the rat within him asked.

"I don't."

"Here, let me help you remember . . ." Puck said, stirring the constellations within the child.

"I remember . . . I remember all of it now," Archie said as the spheres of his eyes turned within their sockets. *The Belly Slitter.*

Steadily coming over the hill like the breaking sun, swaying back and forth so slowly it was almost imperceptible that it was moving. Archie still couldn't make out much from his angle and the shrinking distance between himself and the god, but its size was magnificent, one of legend. Archie's mind pinged back and forth between the minotaur, the Medusa, and now the Belly Slitter—the silhouetted form making shape beneath the tangerine moonlight. It had no eyes, merely a large leathery flesh beak for a face. It had no distinguishable features besides a sharp mouth and very large scissors draped across her back like a traveler's bag. She had a handkerchief hood tied neatly beneath her chin. Archie couldn't tell why, but it seemed feminine to him. It was dressed in old, shabby, dark-gray homespun clothing that was covered in something like soot and an apron that had browned from age and decay. Its skin had a pale, almost translucent hue, and its fingers were thin and flexible. Archie had never had a grand-mother, or seen one for that matter, but he imagined the Belly Slitter was as close to one as he could get. The boy was fully aware, watching intensely as the incarnated deity of terrifying proportions walked the land just as the Greek gods did from Archie's favorite stories. Once the Belly Slitter came to where Archie's body lay beneath the sycamore branches, it opened its large canopy of a mouth and face, letting out a ghostly cry.

Ga ga ga!

"Puck, stop! I don't want to think about this any longer!" Archie said, coming to from his vision in the boiler room.

"Moonchild, you must. There isn't much time, remember?" Puck said, stealing the child's attention and forcing the recollection upon him.

The Belly Slitter let out another shriek, loud enough that even in death Archie could hear it. Then from the school, the snow began to disappear at an alarming rate

251

as the icy white color was replaced by something else. Something was crawling up it—rats. Rats, coming in like a cloud of migrating birds, each one of them racing toward the Belly Slitter's call.

"This was their wish," Puck whispered, back from his vision. "They did not wish to be whole, or to leave, or to be healed. They wished for your loves to be taken by the Belly Slitter."

"Puck, don't show me anymore!" the entranced boy shouted.

Puck waited the full day's turn to be united with the Belly Slitter, and within seconds, Puck became one with the storm of rats below. Like rain falling upon the sea. Puck was gone to the Belly Slitter and its call. Archie watched the vision in horror as the rats beneath the sycamore tree organized themselves into groupings and lines to follow behind the Slitter.

Tears blazed his cheeks, snot oozed from his holes, and blood squirted from his clenched fists. As his eyes continued their rotation in his skull, the disease intensified with his angst as he witnessed the vision. His body continued to cough blood and goo.

The Belly Slitter gazed down at the boy, unmoving.

Studying him with predatorial intensity. The Belly Slitter raised her large finger and pointed at the boy as she began to stomp her feet like a frustrated bird. A knee bent up and slammed down into the powder, over and over. Ga ga ga. A dirt ring formed beneath its feet as it gazed at Archie's body. Its long fingers and arms bent downward through the dirt, scratching the surface, looking for its offering. Ripping it up from the hole, it lifted an earth-crusted liver. Dandelions filled the air, landing in the dead boy's teeth and hair. The Belly Slitter paid no mind to Archie, except for an occasional glance. Then something came that Archie never expected—warmth. He could feel the Belly Slitter inside of him, and his head flooded with words and languages, as if pelicans were released within his skull. The Belly Slitter didn't open her mouth nor speak a word, but Archie understood every last thing she said and wanted. Her voice was too much for any living being to stomach, her grooming too much for his heart. The Belly Slitter tilted its large birdlike head toward the boy and pressed its forehead against his right there in the dirt.

Then, like a collapsing star, Archie returned to the boiler room. His heart beat like thunder, and short breaths came and went as everything he had seen became a reality. Dorothy and Wentworth had taken everything from him. Everything. As Archie's mind swirled with thoughts, Puck intruded, "Not just them, but every child here. Take from them all."

Archie stood on his feet, but his body felt alien to him. He felt remade, salvaged with resurrection bones. But before he could make his way out of the boiler room, the sound of a child's laughter brewed beyond the furnace. He didn't know how he knew who the laughter belonged to, having never heard him before, but a knowing within him took form.

"Francis."

"Hello, Moonchild."

THE BELLY SLITTER

THE CORONER ARRIVED JUST BEFORE DINNER. His white-painted carriage was a stark contrast against the setting purple sky. Children ran from every corner of the school to witness the commotion, all except Wenty and Dot, who knew exactly why they were there. They listened to the pattered footfalls of their peers filling the halls.

"Do you have any tobacco?" Wenty asked, defeated after a long day of searching for their hurting friend.

"Duh," Dot said, taking a small stash from beneath her useless legs.

"Light it for me?" Wenty asked.

Dot, uncaring, ignited the tomato bowl right there in the school's chapel hall. The warm-colored sky illuminated the stained glass, forcing an electric glow. "The sky is beautiful this evening, Wenty. Want me to describe it?"

"Please," Wenty said, resting his head against Dot's shoulder as he inhaled his vice.

"Well, there are pinks, oranges, yellows, and reds," Dot said with her inhale. "Pink looks like love to me. It's bright yet fearless. Then there is orange, a color of riches and—" But before Dot could continue, she felt her blind friend shaking near her. He was sobbing, wetting her shirt.

"We'll try again tomorrow," Dot said to Wentworth. "I promise."

"Do you think we could have saved him if we had made a different wish?" he asked.

"Perhaps, Wenty. Perhaps," Dot said, putting her arms around her friend.

They sat there for what could have been a lifetime. Dot watched the sun fall into the earth, and Wenty listened to her breathe. They were content to rest in this glimmer of normalcy, if even just for a moment.

Wenty wanted to stay for an eternity, but the moment was interrupted by the clanging of the chapel doors opening. It was Giggy. "Hey, Dot."

"This better be important, you nutsack!"

"I just thought you'd want to know that a coroner is here for the bodies. Do you guys want to come and watch and stuff?"

"We know that pig-teeth!" Wenty shouted at the fat boy. "Beat it!"

"Wait, Giggy, did you say *bodies*?"

THE TWO CHILDREN RACED through the hall, making
their way toward the commotion, hoping and praying
they were wrong in their suspicions. They could hear
the murmurings of children rising and falling at the
far end of the school. Their hearts boomed with them
in fear of what they'd find, or rather *who* they'd find.
Just around the corner, they'd finally know. They'd
finally put their bustling nerves at peace. But before
they could arrive, Francis emerged from the library in
a panic, blocking their path.

"Holy shit, you scared me!" Dot said, trying to
make her way around him.

"You must stop him!" Francis demanded.

"We're busy. Get out of the way, Francis,"
Wenty added.

"It's the fat one."

"Giggy?" Dot asked.

"No, the deaf and fat one."

"Archie! What about him?" Wenty said threateningly, relieved that he was alive.

"He's about to make a most terrible decision."

Dot rolled near the fire boy and grabbed his collar, bringing his disfigured face close to hers. "Listen, you shit-puddle, you better stop with the games. Tell us what's going on or we'll find out if your balls can catch on fire too."

Francis smiled. He enjoyed witnessing fear, but there were greater things to worry about at the moment. "He is making a wish."

"How?" Wenty shouted from behind Dot. "How is that possible?"

But before he could reply, a screech came barreling down the hall toward them—an animalistic wail from one of the nuns. Francis couldn't help but smile as Dot released his collar, throwing him back toward the library.

"Who did this?" the nun screamed. Dot and Wenty hurriedly continued down the corridor as Francis followed. "Which monster here could possibly do this?" It was Sister Carrie, holding a rotted baby corpse, cracked open like shellfish.

"Claire! Oh my fucking god. He's making a wish
with Clarie," Dot said, reaching for Wentworth's
hand. Dot, feeling the need to vomit again, wheeled
herself into the nearest bathroom. Before Wenty
could go after her, Francis grabbed his arm.

"Wait, boy."

"Get off of me," Wenty said, jerking his arm back.

"You must stop the wish."

"What is he wishing for exactly?"

Francis made a face so desperate, Wenty felt as
if he could see it. "What is it, Francis?"

"It's for the children. Us. You, the lame girl,"
Francis said, guiding Wenty to the shadows.

"What do you mean?"

"The children, like the rats, to be no more."

Wenty swallowed his tongue at the sound, his
body searching for air to breathe. "When is he plan-
ning on doing this?"

"Now! You must stop him before it's too late!"

"Why didn't you stop him?"

"Don't you think I gave it my all, you fool?" Francis said, digging in his pocket. "He overcame me. His
strength is . . ." Francis was at a loss for words, some-

261

thing rare for the fire boy. "But he'll let you get close to him. Closer than I could get."

For the first time ever, Wenty sensed vulnerability and chose to trust the fire boy.

"Take this, and stick it into his throat," Francis said, placing an injector needle into the blind's boy's hand.

"What is this?"

"Poison."

Wenty wanted to throw it, break it beneath his feet, crush it in his hand, but for some reason, he felt that this might be the only solution if Archie had changed into what Francis was describing.

"Make haste, blind boy, or we'll all share the fate of the rodents."

"EMERALD EYES," the night mother said. "They remind me of the Mediterranean seas."

"Oh my, you are quite right. Those are stunning," Sister Teresa added, waving her fingers at the baby. Each of the sisters cooed and whistled to get the child's attention, both of them desiring to make eye contact with the child. The baby's glance conjured feelings of when one is gazed at by the wild, a fallow or nova.

"When was he dropped off?

"Late last night," the night mother said, wiping the sweet milk from his chin. "The father was willing, but the mother struggled."

The other nun gave the familiar nod of understanding at the statement while attending to the other crying babies. "We're out of cribs in here. Should I wheel in a cot from the eastern wing nursery?"

"No, no, that's unnecessary," the night mother said, picking up the baby to carry him off to sleep. "I was just going to place him in the basket by the fire for now."

"I see. Well, I'm off. Will you be here tonight or retire to your chambers?"

"I'll be in my chambers tonight. I haven't been sleeping too well down here."

"I understand. Blessed sleep, Sister."

"Blessed sleep in Jesus, Sister," the night mother said, giving the baby one last swaddle as she laid him in the wicker basket.

The night mother did one last round to every crib in her stead. Fourteen cribs and fifteen slumbering infants dreaming before God. She blew out the candles, allowing the fire light to glow, and gave one final look as she shut the door on the children. She gave a special, endearing eye to the newest member of Blackburn's, whose name came from the note left with the babe: Wentworth. But before she could shut the heavy door, Sister Teresa returned in a scuffle. "Forgot my prayer book," she said. The night mother gave her a smirk, opened the door for her, and went off to bed herself. "Shut the door tightly, will you, Sister?"

"Of course!" Sister Teresa assured. In her hurry, the nun grabbed her prayer book and quickly made her way to the nursery exit. She did what each of us has done before—a simple mistake, a common accident of forgetfulness—and left a small crack between the door and its jam.

A crack the size of a small rat.

"A WORD, DOROTHY?" the priest asked through sad eyes.

Dot was wheeling out of the washroom with blushed cheeks and a furrowed brow. "Now isn't the best, Father."

"It's regarding Archibald."

Dot halted and submitted, allowing the priest to push her toward his study. The two entered as they had a thousand times before, Dot sitting helplessly and the priest working hard to console her. Many candles were lit, illuminating the study in somber light. Rarely had this many candles been lit in the priest's study, which only added to Dot's worry.

Between the two, words came back and forth like the rising and setting sun, prayers arrowed, rosaries fondled, and tears were cried as the priest gingerly explained in as much detail as needed about

Archie's death and condition. Normally, the priest would never give such graphic news to a child, but Dorothy was no ordinary child, and they both knew that. This was why she possessed a special place in his heart—a seat only a daughter could take.

Dot worked hard to reconcile what she thought she knew of her old friend and the news before her. *Is Francis wrong? Is Francis messing with us? Archie must be gone, but then . . .*

As Dot's mind spiraled, the priest gave one final plea for Dorothy to pray with him.

● ● ●

"Dot! Are you here?" Wenty asked as he opened the washroom door. *Shit!* he said to himself after being met with silence. Wenty poked his cane at the ground as he walked, calling out for the girl. "Dot! Where are you? We gotta hurry!"

"Dorothy is with Father Gregory, Wentworth," an unknown voice said from behind him.

"Okay, thanks," Wenty said, changing his course of direction, picking up speed at the fear of what could be happening to her. This was his chance.

His moment. To undo the terrors that seized her. To be her hero, to be to Dorothy what she'd always been to him.

The blind boy could hear Dot weeping behind closed doors as the priest spoke over her. The door was cracked ever so slightly, allowing Wenty to eavesdrop. But what he heard shredded him.

"Father, don't make me do this," Dot begged as she hugged the old priest. She'd never admit it even to her own heart, but she didn't know where she'd be without the priest's intercession.

"If not for you, then for me," the priest spoke confidently, embracing the girl, a surrogate.

"Father, I can't keep doing this," Dot said. "I so desire to believe," she whispered quietly into his chest, "but . . ."

"I understand," the priest spoke back with fatherly undertones.

Wentworth backed away from the study doors, embittered with rage. Every blood cell in his body felt volcanic, as if his insides were replaced with wild animals. After years of Dot visiting this priest, he finally understood everything as his worst nightmares incarnated right before him. Wenty put his hand over his mouth to conceal his heavy breathing, trying to calm his furious heart. Hearing Dot leaving, not knowing what to do, he hid in the shadows as Dot wheeled herself out and away from the priest, his lair, his sexual dungeon.

"Wentworth! I've been looking for you," the priest said as he closed the door. "I have some rather unfortunate news I'd like to discuss with you."

Wentworth wiped the tears from his cheeks, lifted his chin, and marched into the priest's office. He made sure his grip on the poisonous needle was secure in his pocket. His newfound courage, the wolf heart within him, would not be wasted on livers and broken wishes. He would protect the ones he loved. He would kill whoever harmed the one that held his heart.

"Certainly, Father," Wenty said, guiding himself into the priest's study and closing the door behind him. "I've been meaning to speak with you as well," the blind boy whispered.

We can easily forgive a child who is afraid of the dark;
The real tragedy of life is when men are afraid of the light.

—Plato

DOT ROAMED THE SCHOOL looking for Wenty before abandoning the search and heading into the winter wind. No coat or scarf, no mittens or winter boots. Just Dot and her eagerness to know or understand whatever Archie was now. *Dead? Alive? Both?* Even thinking this to herself, she couldn't help but acknowledge her own change these past couple of weeks. She too oscillated between heaven and hell, some days an angel and others a devil.

She rolled her way through the snowy rocks and tangled weeds. Her hands were freezing as the wheels brought snow with every turn, but her pain was no longer a burden; it was natural. Commonplace. She made her way to the bottom of the hill, looking through the falling snow at the sycamore tree for any sign of a resurrected boy, or a dead one. Remnant hope floated in and out of her like phantoms. But alas, there was nothing, just the winter's snow.

In that moment, Dot did the only thing she felt she could do and relinquished her friend. It was an abortion of the boy who felt like a child to her, uncaging her maternal nature, as if she was a feathered creature. Wiping the cold snow from her hands, she handed him over to the elements and forces beyond her. She looked down at the pact scar on her palm, rubbing it with her frozen fingers, a ghostly reminder of what haunted her. Lengthening her gaze, she could see fading snow prints about a child's size that made their way toward the Wishing Hill. She stared at them, unable to do anything. She knew everything she needed to know in those forsaking steps. Then, like that, it was done. She was almost relieved. She knew stopping him would be no easier than holding back the snow as it fell. So with that, she turned her chair toward the school. Her home. Blackburn's, with its gargoyles and stone pillars that she was more familiar with than her own loved ones.

"Goodbye, Archibald."

• • •

"Wentworth, I have some rather unfortunate news to share with you," the priest said, rolling a cigarette of his own making. Wenty could feel the syringe in his pocket as if it was burning through him.

"Is it about Dorothy?" Wenty asked, adjusting himself in the study's chair.

"In a way, I guess," the priest said, choosing his words carefully.

"I know what you two do together."

The priest halted in motion, confused by the accusatory tone. "Are you referring to our prayer meetings?"

"Is that what you call them?" Wentworth bit back.

The blind boy had the priest's full attention as the meeting was starting to tilt on the other axis. "Now listen, Wentworth, Dorothy means a lot to me, and I will not stand here and—" But the priest's final words never came. They died in his mouth as the poisonous brass injector was forced through at the base of his skull. Its golden rapier lay across the interior of his open mouth, jutting its tip between his lips like a serpent's tongue. The priest looked down in disillusion, coiling his lips around its tip as poison leaked from its hole. He shot around to face the blind boy.

Wenty was breathing hard, not knowing what part of the Father he hit but knowing he made contact. "I'm sorry, I'm sorry, I'm sorry," Wenty mumbled. The priest frantically tried to reach behind his head to pull out the syringe, and the blind boy knew he was in danger of failing in his mission of saving Dot. He quickly raised his cane and swung it in the air, praying to make any sort of contact.

Whack!

The blind boy listened to the priest fall hard on the stone floor like a sack of grain. "Fuck!" Wenty yelled at the situation. The priest was still moving and writhing, attempting an escape. Wenty groped for his cane and jumped in the direction of the dying man's sounds. He landed upon the father, pattering his body in search of both it and the poisonous needle. He worried about getting poked by its stinger, but he found it. It had been plunged further into the back of the priest's head, so he pulled it out and brought it down again hard on the priest's skull. Another strike hit his adam's apple, another in the cheek, then another, then another. He didn't even know where he was hitting anymore.

Wenty whispered and cried to himself, "You can't hurt her anymore. You can't hurt her anymore!" Then, when it felt as if all of the breath had left the priest, Wenty removed the syringe and hid it within the only thing he could find in the blackness—something that felt like a metal box hidden upon the shelves.

Wenty did his best to push the priest beneath his large wooden desk. The priest's body was surprisingly soft and moldable to the boy's push and pull, making the father fit snuggly. The boy wiped his wet, bloodied face with the priest's robes, blew each prayer candle out that he could find, and made sure the study door was locked behind him.

"Goodbye, Father."

THE TWO CHILDREN FACED EACH OTHER in their beds, both aware the other was awake, both beacons of light in each other's darkness. Both were fatigued in their search for hope yet still found enough faith to reach for the other. Wenty stretched his fingers across to the girl's bed, waiting for her to return the gesture. Dot grabbed the blind boy's hand, holding it as if it was a rope out of the miry clay. Neither would say it, but they each knew what would come tonight, how the sun had swirled around their world, how the moon had turned atomic, how the stars had hidden from the Belly Slitter. Nothing would be as it was ever again.

"Do you think it will hurt?" Dot asked Wenty.

"Death?"

"No," Dot said, rubbing her fingers between his. "The call."

Wenty knew what she was asking but allowed his silence to answer.

"Is there a heaven, you think?" Dot asked, trying to fend off her sleepiness.

"Yes, there is a heaven," Wenty said, yawning.

"Can you describe it to me?" Dot asked, releasing Wenty's hand and rolling to her back, perhaps to gaze upward toward what she couldn't let herself want.

"Heaven is a lot like now; red grass, orange skies, oceans made from silver. A place with no winter and chocolate mountains."

Dot smiled at the blind boy's attempt at description. "Keep going," Dot said, losing the battle with her eyelids.

"There will be no shadows, as the light that is God will brighten every corner and secret. Birds will fly low, and butterflies will soar in the clouds. Fruit will grow from stones, and spiders will weave a spiritual tapestry as blood is replaced with honey. New colors that no one can conjure will paint the streets, and I'll be able to see it all. Never blinking so I don't miss any moment, so I don't miss a single crashing wave or budding rose. I will see everything all at once. I will see you, and you will see me. It'll be life, and life abundant." The final words Wenty spoke fizzled out like a forgotten fire. There they slept, unaware of what nightmares lay outside their slumber. Its incarnation perched like a Greylag goose on the northern hill, waiting for the orange moon to form.

"Ga ga ga."

The sound broke into the school's walls like a mist, its gas laying itself upon the children of the school. A dew began to grow on the children as they slept, an acid boiling its way into their hearts and minds.

Wenty awoke first. Not from the noise from the hill but the sound of shuffling in the hallway. A scurrying sound, not unlike that of rodents, bolstered itself in the hallway, growing louder and louder. Then the sound popped around him like embers, the children stirring in undead movements.

"Dot!" Wenty whispered.

"I'm awake."

"It's happening."

G A

G t

GA GaGa

GA GA
GA

The windows vibrated at an extremely fast rate, while the clocks on the wall suddenly stopped ticking. The spiders and moths made their escape for stone crevices they could squeeze into.

"This is it." As Dot spoke, the core of her being moved and pulled herself up, making her stomach twist. "Jesus Christ," she said. She looked at Wentworth, who was doing the same motion, and the next child down, and the next and the next. All stood in unison and faced the recently broken windows, their faces distorted in the moonlight.

"Dot!" Wenty shouted, unable to see if she was okay.

"Try and grab my hand. I'll get to you," Dot said, her maternal nature coming out again.

"I can't move. My body is . . . is . . ." Wenty cried.

"Is his control," Dot said, finishing Wenty's horrible thought. "This must have been how the rats were."

The other children wailed and cried for help. Screams and stomping paraded through the room in perfect unison, but there was no sign of help. Dot watched as her body made several attempts to stand but failed as she fell back on the bed. She looked back at Wentworth for help, only to watch him bash his face against the wall and claw at the wall like a rat.

"Dot, help me! Oh my god, please help!" the boy cried. Tears and blood mixed on his cheeks and forehead.

Dot watched as the blind boy's eyes failed him. His disability blocked his ability to find a way out. She could hear his teeth break against the cold stone of the school, then her head turned toward an open window at the sound.

"*Ga ga ga.*"

Each orphaned child in the room forced themselves through whatever opening was available to them, each of them wailing in terror and pain, pressing themselves against one another, and if the walls were not solid stone they would have pushed themselves through, turning to pink mush in the process.

The other children trampled over Dot as her body tried to move and attempt to pull itself up. Finally her body changed course. Dot felt her body crawl between the other screaming children and up and out the cracked window, landing firmly on the hard snow outside. The window shards cut her stomach and legs, causing her to scream in pain, but then she saw it, the Belly Slitter.

"Ga ga ga."

It was her first time seeing such a deity. Its enormous birdlike shape was terrifying.

From where she lay on the ice, between the other children's parading legs, she could see the glow from the northern hill and two silhouetted figures standing beneath the sycamore. As she neared, the image grew clearer.

She couldn't help but worm herself up the hill in the trampled snow. She felt every movement, the scrapes of pebbles, the chill of the chunky ice, the other children stepping on her knuckles and toes.

There was no sign of Wentworth, as the other children blocked her view completely, they too in an intoxicating trance to meet their master. Dot didn't have time to ask if others were okay, as her concern lay greater in why she had lost all ability to engineer her own being. She was a puppet, a glove, a centipede in a jar.

Her attention was stolen as she came face to face with other crawlers on her right and left. *Infants.* Dozens of babies of all different sizes dragged themselves to the hill, each crying with piercing shrieks, their faces purpled from the cold. Everything inside Dot screamed against the unnatural scene displayed before her—the unnatural movement of infants, their weak necks dragging their large skulls in the powder, making their necks look broken.

The sight of her loved little ones being dragged toward the Belly Slitter made Dot vomit in the snow, warming her chest as she unwillingly crawled over it. She felt the terror of the children marching toward their doom, their bodies determined, their minds resisting. Dot desperately wanted to reach to comfort or hold one of the young ones, but she couldn't. She was not her own.

"Ga ga ga."

The Slitter's song was so enchanting, Dot could feel her mind fading. The vibrations from the Slitter's throat soothed and numbed the children's bones. Dot wanted to turn her head to look back at the school in the hopes of an adult making their way to help. The place that felt like a prison was now her only hope.

The other children passed her quickly and started up the hill with ease, categorizing themselves by gender, age, and size.

"Wentworth, where are you?" she shouted at the bottom of the cold hill.

The horrifying shrieks of children were the only response.

A few of the puppeted infants summited Dot's body and shuffled over her to get to the hill. They wrestled hard against the hills, boulders, snowy banks, and obstacles like Dot's body, which struggled to reach its hellish goal.

Now that she was closer to the Wishing Hill, she could see the figures clearly. The Belly Slitter stood over her servants, horrible and monstrous. But nothing prepared her for what she saw next to the god—Archibald. She couldn't contain herself and roared to her friend, "Archie, you son of a bitch! What did you do? What did you do! Archie!"

From where she lay, she could see Archie staring at her. His eyes almost glowed from the snow's reflective crystals. The shape of his head was bizarre and perverse, a shadow of who he used to be. She couldn't be positive, but she was almost certain he was glaring through his bulbous infected cheeks, grinning like a Halloween pumpkin at what he'd done.

"I fucking hate you, Archie!" A lie she felt in her

gut. Her autonomous body couldn't take that away from her, even as it forced her to lie stomach-down on the ice as the other capable children abandoned her in the snow.

"Ga ga ga."

"Mother! Mother!" Francis shouted from the rows of parading children. "It is I, your servant, your special one."

Francis marched closer to the Belly Slitter, his face void of fear, making him stand out in the ocean of terror surrounding him. More shouts of attention burst from Francis, and Dot could hear his chatter from where she lay at the bottom of the hill.

"Mother, may I join you? I seem to be unable," Francis yelled sheepishly over the cries.

The Belly Slitter pointed its leathery flesh beak and faced the fire boy, cocking its head to acknowledge the child. The god then grabbed Archibald's cold hand and walked over to Francis, approaching the child the way a goose would approach its gosling. A sideways witch stride made even Archie look down to examine her legs beneath the canvas dressing as she moved. They were goblin-yellow and as thick as tree stumps. It was then Archie realized they were bird feet.

"My Lord, my mother, I've done what you asked," Francis said with reverence and emotion-laced relief. "I promised you three broken children, but look! There are more children here than you could ever imagine, livers of all sizes, pink and warm. Have I pleased you, Mother?"

Archibald tugged tightly on the tattered apron of the Belly Slitter, pulling her massive head toward him. Archie gave a secret whisper to the god, and as the birdlike monster listened, its focus never left Francis. It had no eyes on its head, but Francis knew its gaze well.

"You did not do this. These are not yours to claim," Archie said to the fire boy.

Francis could feel his fear taking form, like a fetus inside of him, growing, expanding.

The Belly Slitter dropped Archie's hand and approached Francis, just as she did on the day of his offering—the day his home seized in fire and she formed a new boy from his ashes. The bird god tilted its head slowly, examining Francis, her duckling.

Then she opened her mouth wide, wider than what should be possible. Francis heard the clicks and cracks of the jaw coming apart.

Archie watched in awe, knowing what would happen, his heart coming apart like the first time he felt heard. Seen. Known. This god was his, and he was hers. He had found his home, and it was within the Belly Slitter. Like a pearl harbored within an oyster. His emotions glowed with the embers of relief, a feeling that felt foreign to the plagued orphan.

"Please, Mother," Francis whispered through crispy lips. And in an instant, the Belly Slitter gobbled up the boy. The she-god cocked its head back as Archie watched her swallow the boy in his entirety as he flayed about in her throat, searching for an escape like a carp in the throat of a pelican.

The Belly Slitter clicked her beak as if smacking her lips from the overdone taste of the fire boy. Archie felt a pit in his stomach, fearing his new mother, but that too was outweighed by the new feelings of acceptance.

The other children screamed in panic, wondering if they were the next seeds for the demon bird.

Even after the Belly Slitter had swallowed Francis, the children closest to the monster could hear the swallowed boy's muffled screams from her gut. Francis's cry was harrowing enough to peel one's skin off, inviting greater havoc to the already chaotic scene.

The god grabbed Archie's hand and walked to the front of the march. She let out a final "ga ga ga," and Archie watched as her throat expanded in and out with each cry, an amphibious ballooning of her leathered skin. She looked at Archie, pointed to a distant red star, and led her goslings to their eternal— so the Belly Slitter thought.

There at the bottom of the Wishing Hill, lay the lame girl. Her body jerked for several minutes after hearing the last of the crying children. Once the howls of her peers were but faint whispers, there was silence, with only the wind to interrupt her thoughts. Dot was aware of herself once more and perched herself up on the boulder, looking up at the heavens. She screamed louder than she ever had. Her scream, an electric siren, pierced sharp enough to alert the school staff. Why they didn't come sooner only brought deeper frustration. *Could they not hear?*

Had the Belly Slitter blocked their ears? Are the cries of children lost on them now?

Bringing in the dawn of new mercy, she lay back and reached into her nightgown's pockets. She pulled out her pipe with shaking hands, checked its bowl, and prayed for any amount of tobacco. A single match, broken at the tip, lay at the bottom of her pocket. She dragged it across the boulder and let the ember fall into the bowl, inhaling and calming her nerves.

Then, the invalid fell backward upon the rock and slipped into blackness.

HE HOISTED HIS YOUNG DAUGHTER up on the appaloosa, straddling her tightly between himself and the animal's withers. They took the same trail every Sunday between the east bend and the southern ridge, the one where the rocks "look like robin's eggs," as she'd say in her childlike babbling.

Father would often pack supplies for overnight stays if necessary. Depending on the weather, it could take more than a handful of hours to arrive at the town. Sometimes he would stop to scrounge for rocks, crickets, and even some panning if the stream's flow was right. But the girl was in no hurry. Her advent to these journeys would begin anew at the start of every week. She lived for these moments, as any four-year-old would. The world was theirs, and she knew it. Clouds would greet them and animals would sing and dance. Her father had an excellent voice and she could listen to him sing until daybreak. He'd often sing her to sleep. The vibrations in his chest soothed the sleepy child in his lap.

They made this trip together three hundred and forty times, but this trip—trip three hundred and forty-one—would be their last. This pilgrimage to town for supplies felt foreign, as if her father was not her own. There were no clouds or animals, not even the occasional rabbit. Her father was quiet, sometimes making slight moans from his stomach, clearing his throat too often and stretching his fingers between pulls. Then, on the outskirts of the commune, he died—or so the little girl thought.

Her father fell into a seizure upon the horse, convulsing rapidly, the reigns tied around his wrist. He pulled the large animal on top of him and the daughter he loved. For a brief moment, the three became one, a nest of limbs and bone. The horse, shaken by the sudden rumble, returned to its wildness and bucked. Its power was brought down hard upon the earth beneath it, treading the grass, mud, and skin. The girl's lower spine was crushed into powder, like a flare of dandelions within her.

Her scream, like a siren, agitated the panicked beast, sending it toward the river. The young child tugged and pulled on her father. She scratched at his face, squeezed his hands, and tore at his eyes to no avail. He did not awaken. And he would not awaken until the following evening under the blanket of imminent stars.

The girl, who lost her ability to walk, drug herself to the distant town with only the moon lighting her way. The rocks and soil tore at her stomach and soft skin, turning her raw. Tears were the only water to quench the child's thirst. She couldn't conjure any words to form a prayer. She was useless.

As the child dragged herself up the road, she came upon a living soul and moved toward them like a slow animal. She finally arrived and anguished her weary plea before sliding into sleep. The individual was shocked by the arrival but was all too agreeable to offer help. The priest could see she was helpless and alone.

He quickly scooped the unconscious, broken child into his arms, frightened, confused, but tender. The father looked in every direction for someone to claim the child, but like most children abandoned on the steps of Blackburn's, the priest knew it would be superfluous. Father Gregory brought the child into the hallowed school, fed her, attended to her injuries, and prayed with her. He named her Dorothy, after his mother.

"WE'RE DEEPLY DISTURBED OVER THE NEWS of what has taken place at Blackburn's," the mayor said to the crowd of distraught townspeople. "Obviously we've placed the finest we have on the case, who are doing all they can to discover exactly what transpired." The crowd rustled among themselves, like snakes in a canvas bag, whispering words of rumor and distress. The mayor was uneasy, knowing that if he lost the people's trust, he might also lose his place of power. More and more concerned townsfolk made their way to the bottom of the stone steps, looking up to the mayor, who stood erect in front of the town hall.

"Is it true that the school was sprayed with poison only a couple of days earlier?" An unidentified citizen yelled from the crowd. The murmurings again stirred among them.

"That is true, but we're positive it had nothing to do with the children's disappearance."

"Positive?" someone yelled in disbelief. "How can you be so sure?"

"What if the poison brought some sort of madness to the school?" another shouted.

"If that was the case, then the staff and teachers would also have gone missing, and they are accounted for," the mayor said with false confidence.

"Will the county officials be notified?" another unknown shouted from the back.

"At this time, we're gathering as much information as we can locally before we invite others into the situation. Too much is unknown to invite outside officials. We need more data before we can go broader."

"How many children have gone missing?" a woman shouted in the back. The mayor pretended he didn't hear.

"How many?" another yelled.

"All of them, including the infants," the mayor said despondently.

"That's not entirely true," the nun said, shoving

303

herself in front to be heard. Why else would the mayor invite her there if not to provide details?

"Are there any children who are still there?" an elderly woman in front asked.

"Well, that is the best news we can offer at this trying time," the nun said. "Two children still remain with us."

"Who are they?"

"Why weren't they taken?"

"What do they have to say on the matter?"

"The children are scared and definitely shaken up over the matter. As for what they saw, we're taking our time to give them enough space to process," the nun interjected before the mayor could speak.

"Why didn't the adults help?" one individual from the back yelled.

The nun embarrassed to answer, but vowed to answer honestly, "Our doors were locked shut from the outside with knots and rope. If—"

"We'll be questioning them today for greater clues as to what happened," the mayor said, eyeing the nun out of the corner of his eye, the way a wolf would glare at a hare.

"What the fuck is going on?"

"How can any of this be?"

"Mayor, is this town unsafe?"

"Sister, what did the children see?"

The mayor released his grip from the podium and his glare from the nun, allowing her to answer under his terms.

"Well," the nun said sheepishly before the crowd, "one of the children is blind, and the other is tethered to an invalid's chair. So we have limited knowledge and insight as to what they saw or experienced. Most, if not all, of the other children who are missing were healthy and capable, making this situation that much more—"

"Of a crime! A crime I won't stop seeking justice for as your mayor! This is my vow to you, my people!" the mayor shouted, raising his fist like every ape in leadership. "So get out and vote, or who knows what could come of these poor children," the mayor continued, pushing the nun away from the podium.

As the people fizzled out and the nun headed toward Blackburn's, the mayor grabbed her before she left. "I don't give a shit about your two cripples' processing time. You get them to talk about what happened that night so I can throw this shit sandwich away, do you understand?"

The nun stared back with a small grin. "Just because I wear a habit doesn't mean I'm a pacifist, Mr. Mayor."

"What does that mean?" the mayor asked, smiling. Hoping it was exactly what he thought it was.

"It means my priority is not your election. My priority is the school," the nun said, wrapping a scarf around her neck as she prepared for a long walk.

"Come off your white horse. Don't think I don't know what kind of school you're running!" the mayor said, lighting his cigarette and coming in close. "You don't get it, do you?" the mayor said as if speaking with a dragon charm. "If *I* don't win, *you* don't win. If I lose because of the washpot you call a school, I will take each and every one of you shit-sippers with me," he said, retrohaling his cigarette. "I'll be there later this afternoon, and I like my tea hot," the mayor said, flicking his remaining cigarette at the snowy ground between them.

• • •

The school was quiet, but not with a silence that evokes peace. This was a silence that remained beneath a child's bed, a stillness at the furthest depth of a cavern. A stifling silence that whispers of someone else's presence. No rats within the walls, no children in the halls, just a couple invalids and their shame.

"You wouldn't believe me if I told you," Dot said, cupping her bandaged elbow. The chapel was large, but the crowding nuns made it feel small.

"Well, you better try, because as of now, I'm all you got," the mayor said, sitting in the pew behind her.

"Someone took them."

"Someone took one hundred and fifty children in the middle of the night without alerting the staff?" the mayor asked skeptically.

Dot shrugged as she rubbed her eyes. "See, I told you you wouldn't believe me." She was used to adults not believing her. But knowing she was at the bottom of the pit added an extra layer of anger to the moment. "God, I need a smoke," Dot hissed.

"You what?" Sister Teresa mooed.

"Another time!" the mayor said, realigning the interrogation. "Fine, I'll play along. Tell me who took them, little girl."

"A fucking bird, grandma, beak-face, magical god!" Dot said in a snap, leaning back in her wheelchair and crossing her arms.

The mayor stood from the cold pew, his face not in disbelief but in frustration. He walked to one of Blackburn's intricate stained glass windows. A significant amount of dust and web clouded the beauty of the glass. "I thought there was an understanding, child," he said, sticking his thumb against a sleeping spider and pressing it against the glass until he heard a satisfying crunch. "I help figure this mystery out, and your school doesn't get shut down. Is that making sense?"

"Why do I care what happens to the school? The children are already gone. Let the school burn for all I care." Dot's response raised a clatter among the nuns.

The mayor abandoned his torture of the spider

and circled Dot's chair like a white tip, locking her chair in place, removing hope from the situation.

"What are you doing?"

"Let's play a game . . ."

"I'd like to be done now, Mr. Mayor."

"No no," the mayor said. "It'll be fun! Sisters, would you give us a minute?"

Sister Margaret's eyes became slits at the thought of leaving this man alone with one of their children. "Dorothy, is that okay with you?" the nun asked.

"She'll be fine!" the mayor interjected.

Dot nodded to the sister as they waddled out like crows.

"Now you can be honest with me," the mayor said, placing his hand on Dot's knee. "I know what you need." He reached into his jacket pocket and pulled out a package of loose-leaf tobacco and rolling papers. He spun one for the girl, lit it in his mouth, and handed it to her.

"Thanks."

"See, I'm not so bad," he added, lighting his own, reaching for a communion tray to ash in. "So, someone took the orphans at Blackburn's?"

Dot nodded in agreement as she exhaled.

"And it was a bad person?"

Another nod.

"Did you get a good look at the person?"

"I believe so."

"But it was dark. You were distraught and in pain, and it was snowing, correct?"

Another nod, slower this time. She felt the mayor unwrapping her mind. "So it could have been this magical bird god, or it could have been a man, a masked man, perhaps a plague doctor?"

"But, it wasn't—"

"But, but, but it *was* a plague doctor. They could look like a bird in the dark, could they not?"

"I mean—"

"You're familiar with their apotropaic faces, aren't you?" the mayor interrupted the girl. The mayor brought his hand to the girl's knee, the cherry of his cigarette close to the girl's paralyzed skin. Dot could smell the burning of fabric as the cigarette lay longer than it should have.

"See, we do understand each other," he said excitedly, bringing his cigarette back for another draw. Then in another dig through his oversized winter coat, he pulled out a bit of parchment and a quill. "Now, all I need you to do is write that the plague doctor used his rodent potion to steal your friends from this amazing school. Can you do that for me?"

The mayor's cherry got even closer to the girl's thigh. Dot watched it burn, wanting to feel it, fearful of feeling it. She grinned. She knew this game. She ashed in the communion tray and said, "Mr. Mayor, if you wish to manipulate someone," she took her cigarette and put it out on her own thigh without a moan or sigh, just the sizzle of flesh. "Find someone who isn't an orphaned, chair-ridden, last-remaining fuck at a school made entirely of shit."

Dot watched the mayor's expression change from confidence to condemnation as Dot rolled her chair away from him and strolled toward the chapel exit.

"This is it, you know," the mayor said, making Dot stop in her tracks. "You will be shipped to another orphanage, that blind bat you call a friend will be sailed off to a different school, and everything you know, everything that is your home, will be taken down brick by brick." The mayor stood from the pew, dipped his fingers into the holy water to grease his hair back, and gave one final exhortation. "You can change that. All I need you to do is confirm the plague doctor as the culprit and it'll be taken care of."

Where your fear is, there your task is.

—Carl Jung

WENTY WAS PUTTING ON A NEW SHIRT, one with less nightmare filth, when Dot wheeled in. His hands hadn't stopped trembling, making buttoning his shirt near impossible. "Dot, can you help me?" Wenty said, showing he was struggling to dress.

Dot came close, bent forward, and started to dress him.

"Sister Margaret said they're closing Blackburn's down," Wenty said.

"Yeah, I guess so."

"Which means we will be sent away—like away from each other."

"Yeah, I guess so," Dot said, this time with a greater pause between words and buttoning. "But I guess that's what happens when a hundred kids get killed at a school," she said, trying to toughen up.

"But they weren't killed . . ." Wenty said, almost as a realization.

"They were taken," Dot said, staring at the stem of a bedraggled dandelion—the one Dot put into his shirt pocket days earlier. She was surprised to see it had made it through everything they'd been through these past few days.

"And if they were taken, that means they were taken *somewhere*," Wenty added, turning to face the northern hill, the same direction his peers had been pulled toward the night before.

"Whatever you're thinking about doing, we can't," Dot said, grabbing Wenty's arm. "Not in our condition."

"Why do you think we weren't taken like the others?" Wenty asked, his gaze still in full tilt toward the hill.

"We were. It's just our bodies couldn't keep up."

"Exactly."

"So?"

"So . . . its only power is its lure. Our bodies can't be lured!" Wenty said, getting excited. He palmed his bed for his winter coat and scarf.

"Wenty, what are you doing? Why don't we just tell the mayor and teachers where to go? We won't make it."

"Do you think they'll actually go on a wild goose chase?" Wenty said, putting a heavy blanket on Dot's lap.

Dot had no response. She knew Wentworth was right. Her experience with the mayor was only a shadow indicative of a larger evil. "We don't even know where they went or how to get there!" Dot said as Wenty attempted to wrap a scarf around the girl.

"You're right, we don't know where they ended up, but we know where they started from," the blind boy continued to pack his pockets with trinkets and odd-end things from his nightstand. *My pilgrimage will be as prepared as it can be*, the boy thought. Then, reaching for the curtains, he grabbed one of the rope drape cords and pulled it hard from its hook. He coiled it like a lasso across his chest.

"Wenty, stop! Do you even have a plan once you find the Belly Slitter? You're going to slay it like Saint George?" Dot said through a disillusioned smile. "Wenty, I want to help. I just want to make sure we don't die in the process."

"Fuck, what happened to you?" Wenty said, moving around Dot's chair. "You used to be fearless, and now . . ."

"Say it," Dot said, not seeing the boy behind her. "Go ahead. Say it. Say I'm a coward."

"I didn't mean that. I just . . ."

"I'm not a coward, Wentworth."

"I know you're not."

"Being slow to do wild shit doesn't make someone afraid. It makes them . . ." Dot aborted the point, feeling it die within her.

"It makes them wise," Wenty said, finishing her thought. "And the wisest thing we can do is go after our friends and fight to bring them home, or we'll lose them and each other."

"Jesus, it's not like we can just fight the Belly Slitter."

"No, we can't."

"Then what are we doing?" Dot asked, almost annoyed.

"Not giving up."

Dot turned to face the boy as he pleaded his case.

"We just need to get our friends, and that's something we *can* fight for," Wenty said, heading toward the bedroom door.

After a pause, Dot said, "Don't forget the tobacco. We'll need that." She tossed the leather bag to Wentworth, smacking him in the face. "Oh shit, sorry!"

"You gotta stop tossing things to me."

• • •

The plague doctor counted over three thousand stone bricks alone on the south side of the mayor's office. He watched to make sure the falling snow filled his bootprints before entering the window he had unlatched earlier.

The office was cold, no candles or fireplaces were lit, and the doctor knew it'd be vacant for a while—the mayor and his team were at the election downtown. The doctor took his time. His leather-gloved fingers glided over every knickknack and ledger the mayor's office contained.

The doctor continued his search for holes, crevices, and voids. There he would squirt and spray his poisonous sludge. He ejected large amounts, every bottle he possessed, into every hole he could find. He hummed along to the sound of a pulled syringe as it went in and out, in and out.

The doctor had never done a dosage of this

magnitude before and could feel himself becoming overwhelmed. Cleaning up his discarded bottles and shutting the window behind him, he left the mayor's office graver than he came. A gas chamber for the devil, a hunter's trap for prey, a living artifice.

●　●　●

As the two children summited the northern hill, they could finally see the damage the children's crusade had made. The snow struggled to replace itself after being stomped on by small feet and crawling bodies. Dot stared in disbelief as she saw barefoot footprints peppered in the snow—a child-made path of torture and magic. Dot shuddered at the thought of their suffering. The battling emotions of gratitude and guilt bit and chewed inside her.

Wenty kept walking with his cane like a wintry wizard as he noticed that the ground beneath him felt odd, unnatural. "Dot, what is this?" he asked, poking the ground.

"Dandelions, thousands upon thousands of them," Dot realized.

"Is it only here?"

"Wenty! You're a fucking genius!" Dot yelled, noticing the dandelion trail heading north. Their seeds fluttered upward to the sky, a reverse snow-storm. "It's a path. This must have been where they went!"

Wenty ran behind where Dot was talking and pushed her invalid's chair forward. "Tell me where to push."

"Forward."

• • •

The incumbent mayor and his challenger sat at opposite ends of the town hall. The town judge between them slammed his gavel for quiet. "The votes are in and have been calculated," the judge said, holding the locked box under his arm.

"We know these are dire days, with darker days ahead. That's why this election was of the utmost importance. We need a leader who can bring assurance, not concern, as we navigate these murky waters of modern society," the judge said, taking a small iron key from his robe, allowing the people to bang their fists repeatedly in agreement against the pews. "The next mayor of our great city, by the power of democracy and divine agreement, is . . ."

• • •

The snow was falling harder than it had in the weeks before, a final storm before spring. Dot continued to look behind them as the dandelions they invaded likened to dust, floating upward after every step. They didn't know how far they had marched. Dot knew the sun was getting low, and the freezing throbs of pain in their fingers and hunger pangs in their gut told them everything they needed to know.

"Our trail home is disappearing, Wenty," Dot said, pulling the scarf over her nose for warmth.

"We don't need a trail home, just a direction."

Dot didn't know what that meant, nor did she have the strength to refute it.

"Do you see anything at all?" Wenty yelled between bursts of wind.

"Just dandelions and snow. See, this is what I was saying," Dot said regrettably. "We don't know where they are or how far they went."

Wenty, knowing that was the truth, did the only

thing he knew to do in moments of misery. "Should we pray?" he asked.

According to Dot's memory, it may have been the only time he'd ever asked that. It was a question she would have never thought he would ask, or at least she hoped he wouldn't ever ask. It was the same painful question the priest had asked her for years.

A moment of silence passed, allowing the whirling winter wind to perform its own. Dot was unsure how to get out of the situation, but before she could speak, Wenty had already started. Dot could only listen as the snow removed all other distractions, allowing the prayer to baptize her into hope. Wentworth's words kindled a fire, warming her heart with heavenly thoughts—a heart of stone to a heart of flesh. Cracks formed in her gargoyle skin as if Wenty's prayer were acid.

But Dot couldn't physically hear a word of it. She had no comprehension of his appeal, as if Wenty spoke in an angel tongue, a language only the sera-phim knew. And yet, she knew every word of it. The way a mother knows the coos of her child, Dorothy knew the words of beckoning help of someone capable of things beyond what you can do; something or someone grander than one's strength or intelligence released within her, as if the years of Father Gregory planting seeds had sown themselves to her innards. Vines and veins tangled as if her blood had turned fluorescent, shining through the acid lines that webbed her, breaking free. Dot's sensation of relief halted as Wenty stopped the rocky push of her chair. "Dot? What's up?"

Dorothy came to slowly. "What? What do you mean?"

"You've been muttering to yourself," Wenty said, placing his hands on her shoulder. "You alright?"

Dot wiped the cold tears from her burning eyes. "Yes. I'm more than alright. I'm ready."

Wenty smiled to himself behind Dot, a smile that was just for him.

"Wait," Dot said, grabbing her snow-covered wheels. "Can you hear that?"

Wenty listened hard, then he too heard the sound of crying children.

"Hurry, we're getting close."

• • •

The town hall exploded with applause at the announcement of the new mayor. To them it was something new to be celebrated. To the old mayor, it was an ending. From across the room, he curled his finger, calling Rosemary, as the town meetinghouse buzzed with commotion.

"I need you to go back to my office and grab my concession speech," he said, surprisingly calm for losing the shred of reality he cared for most.

"I'm so sorry about this," Rosemary lied, trying to console the monster within him. She hated the mayor, but not as much as she hated what he could become.

"Not now," he said through glitched teeth and a forced smile. "Make haste and get me my fucking concession." Other townsfolk crowded around him, leaving no room for Rosemary's words. Then, like an arrow shot from a bow, she made her way toward the office.

It was only a few buildings down, but the heavy snowfall made it feel farther. Rosemary stuck her key in the door and jiggled it. It took a few tries due to twilight approaching.

As the secretary entered, she could sense something was off. If questioned, she would be hard-pressed to explain what; it was the little things, parchment unkempt, cabinets and chests cracked slightly, and the smell. Whiffs and scents of bitter and sweet paraded between rooms, stronger in certain areas than others. Allowing her nose to lead her, distracted from the mission, she lit a candle and searched, breathing deeply, allowing the scent to call her to its source. Another deep breath led her to the stony walls and windows. There she could see wet footprints that had made their way through the mayor's office and small driblets from varying holes within the wall and window.

"What in the world?" she said to herself, examining all that was wrong, itching her eyes between blinks. She knew whatever it was could wait. The concession speech was the focus. The quicker the mayor gave his final speech, the quicker she could be rid of him. *Find it and get back to the town hall.* Flipping through papers on the mayor's desk, she coughed and scratched her eyes, moving his large books and maps. Another cough and rub of the throat. Then she found it, but as she went to grab it, she noticed it had small drips of some dark substance, and the longer she stared at them, the more came. Blood oozed from her eyes and nose, waterfalling on the speech, ink mixing with blood and poison. *What is happening to me?*

Rosemary fell hard to the floor, first to her knees, leaning against the mayor's desk, then face-first to the ground, forcing her nose to intrude on her skull, pushing it fully into her face. Rosemary started to weep, as she had done many times in this office, crying to herself, coughing, frothy white sludge exiting her mouth as the orbs of her eyes turned solid red.

Then, like a prayer, a final breath came from her lips and rose to the heavens.

Do the cranes crying out in the high clouds
think it is all their own music?

—Mary Oliver

INVALID

DOT COULD SEE FRESH FOOTPRINTS and tracks carved into the snow. "We're close, Wenty!"

Just the tone of Dot's message gave Wentworth the strength to push faster as Dot continued to yell out directions.

"There! There! Oh my god, Wentworth, I see someone!" Dot said, pushing forward. "It's them! It's them! It's them!" But just as soon as they came near, Wenty stopped hard in the snow. "What are you doing? We're so close. Let's move!" Dot yelled.

"Wait . . . Everyone is still under her control."

Dot realized what could and couldn't be done.

"Her song. It's her hymn that guides them," Wenty said, putting the brakes on Dot's wheelchair.

"What are you doing?" Dot asked, unsure of his plan.

"Leaving the chair."

"Why?"

"So if we fall under her spell, you won't be able to go to her like the others," Wentworth said, taking the old curtain draw cord and knotting it tightly to himself. "Your disability helped you once before. It'll help you again."

Despite their fear, the two held to each other, enjoying the warmth and feel of the other. Wenty tied the other end of the rope to Dot's waist, making sure it didn't hurt her.

"I need you to trust me. We'll walk the rest of the way," Wenty said, dragging his friend through the snow. He walked fast to catch up to his peers and their dying cries.

"Holy fuck, we're actually doing this," Dot said with an underpinning tone of disbelief.

"We are. We have to." But just as Wenty assured her, he scared her. He dropped Dot into the snow beneath them, standing up tall, stiff, in militant form.

"Ga ga ga."

"Wentworth!" Dot cried from the snow, but she became possessed. A worm in the cold. Mechanical, rhythmic pulls dragged her crippled body toward the distant song of the Belly Slitter. The rope tied between them went taut, and soon Wenty's unstoppable body in motion began to tow the girl who couldn't walk.

"Ga ga ga."

"What do we do?" Dot shouted at Wenty, who was only a handful of feet ahead of her.

"Let it take us."

"Then what?" she shouted, but it was useless. They had caught up to the orchard of other children—perfect rows of screaming children, some who had passed on from exertion or exposure but still standing at full attention.

"Why have we stopped?" Wenty asked. Dot was able to pull herself to the side of the crusade. She sat up, squinting hard to see as night rapidly approached. Wenty was unable to move; he was further along. Dot's body still reached for its entranced goal.

"I can't see anything," she said, exhausted. Noticing a large mound of snow, which formed its own small mountain, she climbed it for a better view with the last remaining pulls the spell gave her, liberating the dandelion seeds from their green tethers that perched at the top. There Dorothy saw something too difficult to put into words, a scene so tragic it could steal the breath from your lungs. A vision that encompasses all understanding of how the world should work.

"Ga ga ga."

With its large shears, the Belly Slitter opened each child from groin to throat. A jagged cut, curtains made from soft skin. There she removed their vital organs and livers as if each body was a cornucopia for her taking. Gently laying her prize to the side for later grazing. The pink meat steamed in the cold, like a smoke fire signal.

"Ga ga ga."

Dot watched as the child stood there motionless. He was gone behind the eyes, asleep in Jesus—his body still in full will to the god before it. The Belly Slitter removed feet of earth beneath the child with its massive hands and in a single swiping motion. Then the wretched children would climb into their grave submissively as the Belly Slitter planted cold earth within their open crevices. Stones, pebbles, mud, and silt packed tightly. Once that was handled,

the Belly Slitter would dig through her layers, searching for needle and thread.

"Ga ga ga."

Another swipe of dirt was laid upon their mud
caskets, and the moment the child was hidden beneath snow and earth, dandelions were born upon
the mound in a single motion. Dot counted the
mounds—counting the buried children—from where
the Slitter stood to the one below her very own body.
Dot threw herself from the dandelion grave. "Holy
fuck, holy fuck, holy fuck."

"Ga ga ga"

"God, Dorothy, just tell me, what is it?" Wenty
screamed to the girl.

"She's taking their livers and burying each kid
in the ground."

Wenty felt as if he swallowed his own throat at
her words as the image of what she described formed
in his mind's eye.

"Any sign of Archie?" Wenty asked, trying to
change the subject.

"Not that I can see."

"Ga ga ga."

"What?" Wenty shouted, unable to hear Dot's response over the bird-god's song.

"*I said, not that I can see,*" Dot repeated.

Silence filled the space between the two and was quickly replaced with the sounds of the scissors and screams before them. Cuts and gloopy sounds filled Wenty's ears. "I wish I could move to cover my ears. I can't listen to this."

"Ga ga ga."

Dot felt the same way, giving in to the hopelessness of the moment. She reflected on all that was as she approached all that would be. "I wish Archie was here," she said.

"Me too. Miss that bitch."

The "ga ga ga" grew louder as the Belly Slitter came closer to the remaining children.

"Do you remember when Archie tried to sing in the choir?" Dot asked, laughing to herself.

Wenty couldn't help but chuckle. "Yeah. It sounded like someone was beheading a horse."

"But Sister Teresa didn't have the heart to tell him he sucked, so she just made everyone else in class sing louder."

"The poor idiot didn't have a clue." Wenty laughed.

"Wenty . . ." Dot said, sucking cold air out of the winter sky. "I think I know what to do! You have to sing!"

"What?"

"Ga ga ga."

"You have to make more noise or be louder than the Belly Slitter."

Wenty caught up to speed with Dot's plan. "Shit, shit, shit," he mumbled to himself as he heard the heavy footballs of the Slitter gaining territory.

"Sing!" Dot screamed.

"Ga ga ga."

Wenty shouted with all of his might the only song he knew.

Praise be to Thee, Father and Son,
And Holy Spirit, Three in one;
And may the Son on us bestow
The gifts that from the Spirit flow,
The gifts that from the Spirit flow.

"Ga ga ga."

To no avail, the children were not detoured from the Slitter's song.

"Is anything happening?" Wenty shouted at Dot.

"No. Fuck!" Dot screamed, reaching to see.

"Ga ga ga."

"I'm not loud enough. Dot . . . *sing with me!*"

It was the only situation that could have res-urrected the girl's faith—a place between heaven and hell, where stones are crushed into powder and lightning liquefies the earth. Dot watched her friend shouting, singing, as if the world slowed down, and the snow paused mid-flight. The Slitter's blades drew up and down, back and forth, snipping and opening. Then, like the opening of one's belly, Dot's mouth stretched into a chasm and released the caged robin at the bottom of her well of disbelief—a robin with a broken spirit and a broken spine. To Dot, it felt like hot steam formulated from her throat, music made visible, louder and louder it grew, making Wenty turn and face the girl. Dot was fixated on the Belly Slitter, whose glaring went from its craft to the lame girl peering over the hill. Its long, fleshy beak pointed in her direction like an archer's arrow. It rose to a standing position; its large, yellowed bird legs shook and stomped.

"The screaming!" Wenty shouted, forcing Dot

to pay attention to the silence. No more children were screaming, their postures were broken, and they heard the horrible thud of bodies hitting the icy snow. Even Wenty fell hard. Soon the children pulled themselves up, trying to understand.

The Belly Slitter stood at the front of the crusade, her direction still locked on the girl. She made no move yet. Dot watched it cock its pelican-like head back as its thin-skinned neck jutted and pulsated. She knew what was coming and shouted before the Belly Slitter could, "Cover your ears and sing loud!" Every attuned child squeezed their heads, as if holding them back from a skull pop and sang the first songs that came to mind. The Slitter released its song louder than before, and snow melted around their feet from the friction of its vibrations. Just as Dot opened her eyes, she saw the creature in a full sprint toward her, scissors in hand.

"She's coming for us!" Dot said to Wenty, pulling his hands from his ears.

Wenty shot back around to face the Slitter, stood to his feet, and demanded, "Tell me when it's close!"

"Why?" Dot screamed at the blind boy, the birdgod closing in tighter and tighter to their location.

"Dot, tell me when!"

"Why, god dammit?"

"Dot!"

"Now! She's here, she's here!" Dot screamed, wanting to shield her eyes from whatever his plan was, but her heart wouldn't let her look away. Wentworth dove in front of the oncoming beast, tripping it. His cold body lay trampled underneath the god's prehistoric talons. He brought the monster down hard into the snow inches away from Dorothy, and the Slitter's shears flew across the plain. Wenty was behind her, unmoving, as his body poked out from the snow in an unnatural position. Dot dragged herself as quickly as she could to the blind boy, checking for a breath, a pulse, a spirit.

"Wenty, wake up! Fucking wake up!"

Behind her, the Slitter rose like Lazarus and made another approach to Dorothy, but before it could gobble her like another duckling, the remaining children descended upon the monster.

Children flung to the right and left. Some were swallowed whole while others bit the bird's ankles and wrists. Dorothy listened to the Slitter honk its nasal siren as the children tore her soft gular pouch from beneath her beak.

Dot continued to shake Wentworth as the bombardment unfolded before her. Seeing nothing was working, she lifted her fist high into the air and punched the blind boy as hard as she could. She woke him up from his quiet row to hell with a loud and fearful shock.

"Oh, thank god, Wentworth, you stupid bitch!" Dot said, embracing him, feeling his warmth returning.

"What happened? Where is it?"

Dot looked back at the war, watching her peers lose, bleed, and get chewed, digested, and shit out before her. "We're going to die, Wentworth. She won." Dot said calmly, brushing the dandelions from Wentworth's face. "But at least this way we can be together." Dot lay her head against his chest.

Wenty had nothing to say. He tried to accept his new reality as his blood painted the ground beneath him, the snow melting and mixing with his red flow, exhibiting the winter grass beneath, which was a shade of maroon. Dot pulled his body closer to her unfeeling legs, resting his head against her chest, letting him bleed on her. Dot looked up to the air for God's intervention and was met with an orange sun. Then, and only then, she realized . . . Wenty's vision. His goddamn vision, its fruition, its becoming here at the moment where it seemed the gates of hell had been pried opened and all of its horrors and devils had been released upon Blackburn's.

"Wenty, your vision, *red grass*, *orange light*!" She said, tearing his eye bandage from his face. "Do you see it?"

"I can see it!" he whispered through coughs of blood.

The words she thought she'd never hear from a blind boy, *I see it.* This only wrung out the remaining tears from Dot's heart.

"Now I get to watch you run," Wenty said, his legs bumping against something cold and metal. Wentworth reached with his remaining strength for the Belly Slitter's nearby shears pooled in his own blood. He brought them swiftly down on his soft skin, puncturing his stomach, making a zagging edge toward his feet, and fell limp. A ritual on his terms, a gospel sacrifice, a lamb to his own slaughter. Dot

341

screamed in panic, trying to push his skin flaps back together, his innards trying to make their way out like the demons in hell, and blood so rich it appeared black. "No, no, no," Dot groaned to herself so quietly she could hear the Belly Slitter fend off the remaining children, wanting her and only her. Its stomps and vibrations rippled Wenty's blood.

"I love you, Wentworth," she cried softly, laying him in the bloodied grass. His eyes were open. Eyes that should not be there, eyes that were stolen from him, ensconced perfectly within him. Emerald green stained glass windows to the soul of the only boy she would ever love.

Not looking away from his eyes, her hands slipped into his wound and pulled out his liver. She freed it, raised it, and brought it down hard into the melted snow. Dot covered it with blood, dirt, and ice, giving the boy back to the dust from whence he came. The Belly Slitter was running toward her, her huge shredded beak agape and hungry. Fast, hard, determined.

Dot turned to face the fucking bird, and through three undertoned mutters . . .

"I wish for you to leave us."

"I wish for you to leave us."

"I wish for you to leave us."

Only inches away from its prey, the Belly Slitter erupted into a constellation of dandelions. A storm of white florets whirled and danced upon the red snow, flickering in tangerine light. Dot would have rather been swallowed, digested, and sprayed out like the rest of her meals, to meet her own death rather than live this life without Wenty. Without family.

But then it would have all been a waste.

A disregarded offering, a dove with no wings, a sun with no warmth . . . and that would have been too much to bear in eternity. Dot knew in her spirit that Wenty's vision was only partial, a half-truth. Dot could not run. Was that what Wenty wanted with his sacrifice? For Dot to wish for herself to escape on her own legs? Thoughts of wonderment, regret, and uncertainty bewitched her mind.

She wiped away Wenty's blood from her face as tears replaced it. Wenty's blood worked like glue on the sailing dandelions. The girl who couldn't walk reached for the Slitter's large scissors as she readjusted herself to cut the cold ground. There she sliced and scooped and pulled the dirt away when it was soft enough, making a shallow grave for her friend. After one final kiss on his cheek, she laid him to eternal rest. Blessed sleep.

Dot dragged herself to the remaining broken children who waited across the pasture for their shepherd. Like Jacob's Ladder, she climbed the terrain closer to something greater, a new life. Not the life she wanted or even expected, but the life she was given. An unforeseen gift masked in defect, weakness as strength, a moon-lit dawn. For this, she cried tears of gratitude as the fistfuls of snow melted with her every push toward the other children.

KNOCK

KNOCK

KNOCK

It felt odd to knock on Blackburn's doors after decades of entering at her own will, but she was no longer part of the sisterhood. She was a civilian, still a woman of God, but no longer a night mother. This brought her relief and grief within the same sting.

"Well, hello, Sister." Sister Margaret caught her old habit. "It's so wonderful to see you again. Do come in."

"Thank you, Sister Margaret," the night mother said, shaking the snow from her boots. "It seems to be warming up outside, doesn't it?"

"Yes, I believe spring is just around the corner."

"Indeed, I always loved Blackburn's in the spring. The garden especially."

Sister Margaret gave a warm nod, then waited for the purpose of the visit to be revealed.

"Yes, right. Is Father Gregory around? I'd love to speak with him regarding his letter."

Sister Margaret did the sign of the cross across her breast and kissed her silver crucifix.

"Oh dear, what happened?" the night mother asked.

"Father Gregory is no longer with us. There has been a horrible accident."

"Oh no," the night mother said, grabbing a handkerchief from her bag.

"It happened the night the children went missing. We're confident whatever took them first attacked him. He loved those children so."

"My heart is shattered," the night mother said. "How will you carry on?"

"Well," the nun said, trying to gain composure, "the diocese has been informed, and they're sending a new priest in April, right before Easter."

"Very good," the night mother said somberly.

"You mentioned a letter?" Sister Margaret asked, wiping her eyes.

"Yes. Father had asked me to come and revisit my role here at Blackburn's—"

"Oh, that would be wonderful!" the nun interrupted.

The night mother raised her hand to stop the celebration. "No, I will not be returning to Blackburn's. I'm leaving the country. It's far too dangerous."

"Then, in regards to your visit?"

"I'm here for Dorothy."

"Dorothy?"

"Yes, I'm here to adopt her as my own. Where is she? I'd love to see her."

Blessed is the nightbird that sings for joy and not to be heard

—M. Rubin

THE SURVIVING CHILDREN CARRIED THE GIRL
who couldn't walk, placing her in a royal position,
high above the melting snow. One of the children
looked over the empty country and asked, "Which
way home?"

We only need a direction, Dot thought to herself.
"South."

The walk home took two days, but there was no
carping among the survivors—just singing.

There was no food in their bellies, but they
were satisfied. Nourished. Content. As they grew
nearer, the clouds pulled back like curtains, allowing
a glimmer of sunlight to fill the valley. They helped
Dot into her chair as the children approached the
northern hill of Blackburn's. Dot stopped the song,
and they watched as the dandelions burst, chimneys
blew their smoke, and the dogwood trees waved

them home. Dot took her pipe from the pouch of her chair and lit a match.

"We made it," one child cried out in the back, allowing other children to join in the celebratory murmurings, some even shouting for pancakes and tea.

Dot smiled in accomplishment and squeezed the hands of the children who pushed her this far. Between her tobacco exhales, she offered gentle nods and encouragement as they continued down the hill where it all started. One of them turned to the girl who couldn't walk, who remained at the top of the hill.

"You coming, Dorothy?"

Dot looked at Blackburn's, then looked over her shoulder at the fresh springtime path. She took a large drag and exhaled into the warm air with a smile.

EPILOGUE

THE DOORS OPENED at St. Hamelin's Boarding School as the teacher encouraged the children to sit up and make themselves presentable.

"We have a new student today, children," the teacher said with enthusiasm. "He is a survivor of the recent attack at Blackburn's that we've all heard so much about." She made her way to the door. "Let's all welcome Archibald!"

Archie entered the classroom, bandaged; his body hung from crutches. His face was wrapped like an Egyptian corpse, shielding his plagued skin from the sun. From the truth. The children gasped at the sight of him. An audible silence floated through the room as Archie hobbled to his chair between two other children. They were perfectly dressed in their collars and pleats, and Archie was stained in filth and pus. His scent was more animal-like than human, forcing his neighbors to hide their faces. The teacher continued her lesson with a smile, ignorant to her pupils, as Archie leaned over to one of them and asked, "Tell me, what do you wish for?"

Scan the QR code to read the poem.

Acknowledgments

First, to you the reader. Whether you liked this book or hated it, I'm grateful you took a chance to read it.

Second, to the horror community, and their unparalleled support. Any success my books have, is largely due to your effort, kindness and zeal.

Third to those who read it (in its unedited and raw state) before its release...Phil, Colin, Ryan and T. You took me out of my funk, and told me to release the friggin' thing, I'm glad I listened.

Lastly, to my encouraging wife, Emily. You've never once looked at me twice with these outlandish storytelling ventures, which was all the fuel I needed to try. Thank you for never doubting, and always pushing.

Albatross Book Co. is a book craft and boutique publishing house.
We are a one stop shop for all your needs to make your book a reality.

——————— *albatrossbookco.com* ———————

Other recent published works include:

SOON TO BE
A MAJOR MOTION
PICTURE!

A FiG FoR All tHe DEViLs

An abused, grief-stricken, and impoverished Sonny has all
but given up on life. That is, until he meets death, by way
of the Grim Reaper. The Reaper, a junk food loving, poetry
reading, cigarette-addicted entity, has no time to waste as
he searches for a suitable successor who would become
"Death" for the next millennium. By training the boy in
the ways of death and dying, Reaper grooms his young
apprentice and through suspenseful and horror-laced events,
he unknowingly gives Sonny something he never intended:
A reason to live.

WINNER OF BEST IN HORROR

Other recent published works include:

A SHORT STORY

"Does the seed know it must die?"

One of Rosemary's final requests of her husband was to create the garden of her dreams. A place where she could live the remainder of her days in peace. A place that will remind her of her best moments and memories long past. Thomas toils day and night to complete it, but in a moment of carelessness in the cabbage patch, he unknowingly rips the veil between the natural and unnatural. What was meant to be a gift rapidly blossoms into an overwhelming curse—one that unleashes a cornucopia of dread, tension, and fraught.

In this short story, C.S. Fritz carries the reader into the dark powers of unresolved resentment, lore, and where hope becomes horror.

Printed in Dunstable, United Kingdom

67408414R00214